ISMAT CHUGHTAI was born i
among the earliest and foremost ·
on women's issues with a directı
Urdu literature among writers of I
several collections of short stories,
Crooked Line), a collection of reminiscences and essays, *My Friend,
My Enemy,* and a memoir, *Kaghazi Hai Perahan* (The Paper-thin
Garment). With her husband, Shahid Latif, a film director, she
produced and co-directed six films, and produced a further six,
independently, after his death.

TAHIRA NAQVI, a translator of Urdu fiction and prose, taught
English for twenty years, has taught Urdu at Columbia, and now
heads the Urdu programme at New York University. She has
translated Ismat Chughtai's short stories, her novel and her essays.
She has also translated the works of Khadija Mastur, Sa'dat Hasan
Manto and Munshi Premchand. Naqvi also writes fiction in English.
She has published two collections of short fiction, *Attar of Roses and
Other Stories of Pakistan* and *Dying in a Strange Country*. Her short
stories have been widely anthologized.

The Heart Breaks Free
&
The Wild One

ISMAT CHUGHTAI

Translated from Urdu by
Tahira Naqvi

women
UNLIMITED
an associate of
kali for women

SPEAKING
TIGER

WOMEN UNLIMITED
(an associate of Kali for Women)
7/10, Sarvapriya Vihar, First Floor
New Delhi – 110016, India

SPEAKING TIGER PUBLISHING PVT. LTD
4381/4, Ansari Road, Daryaganj
New Delhi – 110002

The Heart Breaks Free and *The Wild One* were first published in
English in India as part of *A Chughtai Quartet* by Women Unlimited,
an associate of Kali for Women, 2014
This edition jointly published in paperback by Speaking Tiger and
Women Unlimited 2019

ISBN: 978-93-88326-86-5
eISBN: 978-93-88326-43-8

10 9 8 7 6 5 4 3 2 1

Typeset in Adobe Caslon Pro by Jojy Philip

Printed at Sanat Printers, Kundli, Haryana

The Heart Breaks Free
(*Dil ki Duniya*)

What a strange and mysterious moment it is when you suddenly open your eyes and can't tell whether the sun is setting or just rising, which way your feet are or where your head is, and you don't know where you slept and what this place is where you've awakened! It becomes imperative then, to determine where your head and feet are, and you have this feeling that if you don't find out immediately you'll be lost forever.

When we were children our first reaction to this was tears, but then a flash came down from some unknown source and right away we were able to place ourselves, to determine where everything was. All at once fountains of mirth burst forth, and to provide further proof of our existence we ran after the chickens or began grappling with one another like dogs. At that point Amma would order us to make ourselves scarce and this we happily did. Making a run for the garden we proceeded to pluck off half-opened buds from the bushes and gathered them in our laps.

Thus we occupied ourselves until it got dark. Then Ali Bakhsh would slip in a bunch of lanterns from behind the curtain on the front door. The wicks were raised and lighted and the lanterns dispatched to every corner of the house so that the walls and doors which had been engulfed in darkness were visible again.

The watchman climbed a ladder and lighted the boxed lamp on the front door. Frightened, the bushes hastily retreated into the darkness and the buds we had collected in our laps began to flower. At that time, and for no apparent reason, we were assailed by feelings of dread. A stealthy chameleon, its checks ballooning as it manufactured poison it its mouth, turned red like an ember and then scampered up the tamarind tree. And we felt as if our feet were melting like wax.

This was when that mysterious voice floated and vibrated as it travelled across the water:

"Kanhayya, your flute has become my enemy…"

We ran without a moment wasted, dashed through the curtain on the front door, threw the flowers down on our grandmother's prayer mat and took refuge under her dupatta.

"Dadima, please read ayat-ul kursi quickly and blow on us!"

Only when we felt Dadima's "Ahmed Hussain, Dildar Hussain," soaked in tobacco and betel juice blow on our faces did we breathe sighs of relief.

"*Kanhayya…yo…u…r…flooote…has become my…enemy…*" The sound weakened and then disappeared altogether, leaving behind only the rustling of the wind.

Our father had recently been transferred to Bahraich. Situated across from our spacious, two-storied bungalow was the shrine of Sayyed Salar Masud Ghazi. Adjacent to the house was a garden where we spent the major part of our waking lives. At the end of a long line of modest-sized quarters was a white mosque and rows of har-singhar, jasmine, chameli and mogra trees that extended as far as the eye could see. Not too far from the mosque was a Muslim cemetery and on the banks of the river, some distance away from the mosque, beyond the melon plantation, was a crematorium. We dreaded these two spots the most. The mysterious voice appeared to come from this direction and anything coming from there struck fear in our hearts.

Whenever we stepped out of line, or if we made a row, we were frightened into docility by references to that voice. "She's a demon, she'll eat you up alive, she's a ghoul, if she lays hands on you she'll cast a spell on you. Don't you know what they say? A wedding party once drowned in the Ghagra stream but the bride didn't die, she turned into a demon and floats about in the stream to this day."

There was another factor associated with this voice. No sooner was it heard than Aunt Qudsia suffered a paroxysm; her jaw locked, she'd begin to foam at the mouth and the house turned into an abode of anguish.

"O Mighty Qadir, bring us Qudsia's husband," Nani Bi (our maternal grandmother) chanted, swaying. But Mighty Qadir seemed to have clogged his ears with oil; he paid no heed to anyone's pleas. Perhaps he was ruminating on the matter of returning Aunt Qudsia's husband to her.

She had been married for nearly ten years. Her father packed her husband off to England soon after the wedding—that was one of the conditions of the marriage. In keeping with custom, he returned from there with an English wife, a mem. Now he had a clinic in Mainpuri. This is why Aunt Qudsia endlessly chanted verses from the Quran, spent long hours in worship and prayer, and when all of this proved fruitless, suffered from attacks in which her jaw locked and foam gathered at her mouth. Unfortunate woman, what else could she do? She penned several letters beginning, "My master, may you live long." She wrote: "Give me a spot in a corner of your house as a maid of the Memsahib, I'll serve you both, I'll eat your left-overs, wear your cast-offs, and if I utter one word of dissatisfaction, you may punish me as one punishes a thief. You are the master, I your slave, what better fate can I ask for than dying at your feet," etc., etc.; but the master apparently thought it foolish to bother with a reply.

Usually Aunt Qudsia was introduced to people like this: "This is Qudsia, her husband has taken in a white woman." People were quite impressed. At that moment Aunt Qudsia, too, would forget her misfortune and experience a certain degree of pride. Her rival was the daughter of the rulers, who knows, maybe she was even distantly related to the King! Not everyone can take in a white woman. In a way her husband had honoured her by bringing a white woman to be her rival; he could have taken in a washer-woman or a sweeperess.

Aunt Qudsia was married at the age of fifteen. Six months after the wedding her husband left for England. For two years a fervid romance flourished. Her face lowered, she was seen either writing to her husband or reading one of his letters. Gradually the letters cooled off. She continued her frenzied writing but replies there were none! Then all kinds of bad news started trickling in. After the First World War white women diminished in value and whoever went abroad returned with a catch from the free-flowing Ganga. But Aunt

Qudsia's husband turned out to be rather strange. There were other men as well who were bringing home white women, but once every six or seven months they also showed their faces to their Hindustani wives. Her husband, on the other hand, maintained absolute silence and made no effort to find out how she was doing.

And that's why Aunt Qudsia became hysterical during Urs (the celebrations at the shrine), that's why whenever there was a wedding in the neighbourhood her jaw locked, or when, in the darkness of night, someone sang a song of separation, she frothed at the mouth. The mysterious voice affected her the most, so much so that she paced restlessly, cracked her knuckles, nervously twisted the corners of her dupatta, and suffered an attack of hysterics.

~

We were picking off buds. Our laps were full, but we lingered to see the lighting of the boxed lamp on the front door. Suddenly the voice floated up right behind us. Our hair stood on end. We turned in surprise. She was sitting on a fallen fig tree trunk that had come down during a storm and now lay among crumbling gravestones in the cemetery behind the mosque. Her face wore a sad look. She paused in her singing. Our feet weighed heavily like sacks stuffed with straw.

"Let go of my dupatta," she murmured petulantly, as if addressing someone behind her.

Terrified, we ran wildly from there. No one was holding her dupatta, there was no one there.

She stood up hastily, and tugging at a corner of her dupatta ran away laughing, as though she were being pursued playfully. Soon she had disappeared into the trees.

Fear gripped us, our feet seemed to drag us down.

"We'll meet in Meerut." Her voice echoed in the distance and we ducked around the curtain and into the house.

"You, beloved, so dark, and I so fair/ We shall gaze at each other in the mirror."

Her voice vibrated again like a top and we felt as if there were beadwork-needless running down our backs.

"You, beloved, so stout, and I so thin/ On scales we shall both be weighed."

What a coincidence! Aunt Qudsia's husband was both stout and dark, but there was not a ghost of a chance of meeting him in Meerut. What could she do except have an attack of hysteria?

Nani Biwi was busy with something else. Dadima, who was still murmuring over her prayer beads, blew on us, but our fear did not abate. Uff! How many grandmothers there were, and aunts, both maternal and paternal, but what good were they? There was no vigour in their blowing.

"Stay away from her, child," the attendant at the shrine said one Thursday when we arrived there with our usual offering of flowers. "She's very dangerous."

"Why?"

"She brings bad luck, she ate up her parents and her husband."

"She ate them?" We thought she had sprinkled salt and pepper on them and really eaten them.

"If she catches you alone she'll pull out your heart and eat it," he frightened us further.

"Is she a demon?"

"Of course."

"May God help us!" Chacha Mian, who had come with us, interjected. "What nonsense is this. No, dear children, she's just insane." He glared threateningly at the attendant.

"Insane?" We didn't like Chacha Mian's explanation. All the romance was gone. She's just insane? And not insane in an amusing way either, she doesn't smell or rip her clothes, nor does she throw stones at anyone. Instead, whenever you chance to run into her you find her singing.

"Beloved, I'll be a flower in your lap/ A flower in your lap, beloved."

What a melodious voice. That's why Aunt Qudsia became so agitated when she heard her sing.

"Amma dear, please send for her, we'll hear her sing."

"No, child, I'm not going to send for that mad wretch. She's from a good family and look how she wanders all over the place without restraint, her parda forgotten. She's possessed, you know; everyone drowned in the Ghagra stream, but she remained afloat for three days as if there was something holding her up."

"But the unhappy creature sings well." Aunt Qudsia nursed an obsession for songs. When Uncle Shabir sang devotional songs, streams and rivulets flowed from her eyes.

"*O Rasul-e-Arabi? To you I offer my life,*" he sang and Aunt Qudsia, her dupatta held to her nose, sobbed as she swayed to the rhythm of his song. Everyone sat at attention, waiting for the paroxysm that invariably overtook her when Uncle Shabir sang. Her hands would rotate, her eyes roll up in their sockets, and foam bubble at her mouth. Nani Biwi and Dadima would run towards her, blow holy incantations on her while Uncle Shabir, seated on the wooden divan, tried to conceal the shaking of his hands. Until Aunt Qudsia calmed down, he would pace up and down outside the front door.

Uncle Shabir was related to Aunt Qudsia by marriage, he was a brother-in-law. The only child of poor parents, he was a timid, uninteresting and ineffectual man, and it was indeed lucky he was an only child or we might have had to contend with several uninteresting and ineffectual uncles instead of one. He was very thin and nearly three feet taller than Aunt Qudsia. Humped over like a camel, he was in the habit of taking long strides when he walked.

"Shabir Bhai, please sing something," Aunt Qudsia would entreat in a melancholy voice, "please, it will calm my nerves."

"What can I sing, I have a scratchy throat today." He always presented the same excuse. Then he cleared his throat, blinked his eyes a few times, flared his nostrils, pressed both hands together between his knees, and:

"*O east wind, if you travel to Tayyabba / Promise that you will embrace the curtains of the sanctuary.*"

He sang in a clear, unsullied voice. You felt sorry for him. The east wind had also clogged its ears with oil it seemed; it didn't hear him nor did it travel to Tayyabba at his behest. It was common knowledge that Uncle Shabir was in love with Aunt Qudsia. But what a sluggish, timid love it was. Other young men and women in the family also loved, and what a sprightly and energetic love it was! Amorous embraces in secret or a tussle during a game of pachisi, grabbing hold of each other in dark corners! Grandmothers, uncles and various aunts cursed and remonstrated endlessly but the laughter and giggling continued unchecked.

Uncle Shabir, on the other hand, never sat close to her, never allowed even his little finger to touch her; she was forbidden fruit which belonged to another, to a man who had put her somewhere and forgotten about her. She had recently turned twenty-five and already there were silver strands gleaming in her hair. Everyone hoped she would age quickly so that the matter would end once and for all.

"No, I'm not going near that mad wretch," the old smelly crone, Pathani Bua, retorted when Aunt Qudsia solicited her help. "That husband-eater threatens you with a stone every time you go near her."

"What's amazing is that the ruffians out there don't harass her. If it had been some other girl she'd be in shreds by now. The wretch, she roams around in the woods all night dressed up in her finery. Isn't she scared?" Chachi Bi asked.

"Why, what's she got to be scared of?" Pathani Bua said, "No one dares to look at her with a crooked eye."

"Why? Is she a lioness, will she tear you to pieces? She's always alone, isn't she?"

"No, she's not alone, her husband is with her."

"What husband?"

"Bale Mian…"

"What nonsense! Don't be a fool, woman."

"This isn't nonsense, I swear she's the beloved of her husband, she's a true faithful of our Ghazi Mian."

Pathani Bua proceeded to explain in greater detail. She was Ghazi Mian's beloved, and this despite the fact that Ghazi Mian was martyred four hundred years ago. Love is not fettered by the chains of time.

There was an Urs at Ghazi Mian's shrine every year. Qawwali singers and others came from far and wide. People of every religion and caste, old and young, children, women and men, all made the pilgrimage to the shrine. Offered vows and received answers to their prayers.

Every Thursday the dancing girls from the town and its neighbouring districts arrived with their offerings. They sang thumris, dadras and ghazals in honour of Ghazi Mian. When a dancing girl was about to surrender her virginity she would first sing and dance at Mian's shrine. A fair was held during the flame-ridden heat of May and June, and the faithful came months ahead of time and set up camp. Such enormous crowds gathered during the actual days of the fair that you couldn't find an empty spot anywhere. Stretched in front of the main entrance to the shrine was an over-sized shamiana on which the arriving pilgrims threw garlands, sweetmeats and money.

Flags were transported here from neighbouring towns and districts. There were sixty-foot high bamboo poles with clusters of black or white hair attached to the top, while below them hung streamers made from rupee notes. Anyone whose wish was granted offered the standard at the shrine. Dancing and leaping to the beat of kettle-drums, the men arrived at the entrance of the shrine and formed a circle; a muscular man built like a wrestler, balancing the standard, stationed himself in the middle of the circle; in order to keep the banner steady, to prevent it from tipping, four other men held on to ropes extending from the spire of the standard. Then, lifting up the standard, the man danced and executed tricks with it. Sometimes he'd place the base of the standard on his forehead and wriggle his body, at other times he'd catch it between his teeth and sway. Finally, when everyone began sweating, or maybe when the group ran out of time (there were other groups with standards waiting their turn), the weary flag was furled around the pole like a sail tied to its mast, hitched on shoulders and carried into the shrine through the tall entrance-way.

And then another flag dance began. At the end of the fair days all the flags were auctioned off.

Our mother bought flags every year for use as floor cloths—these were the best examples of tambour-work. Embroidered on the rough cotton fabric were colourful designs in the shape of elephants and horses. Here you could see whole armies on the march with their spears hoisted, there a caravan of camels; in another corner were flocks of sheep and goats, herds of cows, along with groups of men and women exchanging secrets. We would roll around on the divans all day long, observing the scenes below us, never tiring of what we saw.

Besides the flags, those whose prayers had been heard also offered, in accordance with what they had promised, gold and silver figurines, tables, chairs, beds, and pots and pans. All this was followed by Ghazi Mian's wedding ceremonies. A kettle-drum was placed at the entrance. Early in the morning the playing of the drum commenced to one's annoyance and continued late into the night. All day, one group after another came and surrounded the drum players, and sometimes one or two men broke into sad songs about lost love. As soon as one group had exhausted itself another took its place. Women possessed by evil spirits came to Mian's door to be rid of them; they loosened their hair and shook their heads rhythmically from side to side, and when the person chanting holy verses blew smoke over them, they screamed and fainted. But it wasn't long before they regained consciousness and started swaying again. If the spirit were a stubborn creature it would not budge for days; red and green clubs were used to punish it and only then, after a terrible struggle, did it depart. Happy and contented, the women who had been healed then made offering at the shrine and went their way.

On the fifth of the month came the ceremony of the fan, on the seventh the sandalwood ceremony and on the ninth, the henna ceremony. At night on that day, Ghazi Mian's kurta, on which the Quran was etched in its entirety, was brought out for viewing. Frenzied crowds engulfed it. On the eleventh day, the ceremony marking the readying of the marriage procession took place.

A long time ago, Radha Bai, alias Zehra Bibi, a child widow from a family in Raduli, lost her heart to Mian. Ghazi Mian appeared to her in a dream and accepted her love. She made her home in his shrine. She was known to wash the tomb with her tears and sweep the floor of the shrine with her hair every day. Her father was an oil merchant. He forcibly dragged her away from Ghazi Mian, but Radha refused to give in. All girls with the name 'Radha' are stubborn; boldly and fearlessly they announce their love, suffer every dishonour and stigma happily, and put life and soul on the line. And the dice rolls in their favour. Unfavourable winds are compelled to give in when confronted with the ardour of their love, people begin to worship them, sing songs about them, and finally worship them as goddesses.

Ghazi Mian's Radha also had to walk on coals. She too had to drag herself through thorns. Her mother beat her senseless, her father whipped her with moistened rope and tied her to a peg in the cowshed. And the whole village spat at her. In the middle of the night when poor Radha, starving and thirsty, weary from her wounds and splattered with cow-dung, was taking her last breath, Ghazi Mian came to her. He washed her wounds with his tears, clasped her to his sacred chest, and dipping his forefinger into his heart's blood, he made the bridal mark in the parting of her hair.

When the demented Meera fell in love with her Girdhar Gopal the world let vipers loose on her life and gave her a cup of poison to drink and then—Krishan Murari's flute came to life and the viper turned into a garland of flowers, the cup of poison brimmed over with the elixir of life.

The next morning the inhabitants of Raduli awoke to the sound of temple bells and the azan echoing from the minaret of the mosque. Immersed in the fragrance of sandalwood, dressed in majestic clothes, Radha lay on a bed of flowers in everlasting sleep. There was not a single scratch on her, her body glowed like burnished gold, her hair shone with sindhur.

People in Raduli were thunderstruck. A meeting of the village elders was called. It was decided that the girl now belonged in another's house, there was no reason for her to stay in her parent's home. So she was delivered to her groom's dwelling.

The Hindus called her Radha, the Muslims referred to her as Zehra Bibi. Her plain, unpretentious grave sat at the foot of Mian's tomb. At one end of her grave grew a tamarind tree whose bark was known to exude the fragrance of sandalwood when burnt.

Since Radha's death, the Raduliwallahs had been bringing an offering of Mian's barat to the shrine every year. Children were put to bed early so they could be aroused around three o'clock at night to witness the arrival of the wedding procession. As soon as the familiar sound of trumpets was heard everyone was awakened. Quickly splashing some water on our faces, we all ran up to the roof to see the wedding procession enter the village.

It's been so many years, but to this day my eyes are blinded with the memory of that barat. A white steed in front, heavily laden with silver and gold ornaments, covered with flowers, the silvery strands of the sehra kissing the hooves.

"Look, there's Bale Mian!" We thought we could really see him seated on the horse.

Behind the horse was a palanquin with fine red muslin curtains, and inside it was the Quran with a candle burning alongside it.

"The bride, the bride!" We were spellbound. The trembling flame of the candle behind the red muslin curtains appeared to take the form of a shy, reticent bride. Following the bride were the wedding guests carrying tiny umbrellas. These were decorated with small stars between embroidered bands, and beaded silver and gold tassels hung from their edges. Twirling these umbrellas like reels, swaying, dancing, the members of the wedding procession filled the streets. It was a dazzling sight. For days afterwards little umbrellas continued to dance in my vision.

Sometimes, when you see something very beautiful you feel a lump in your throat. Aunt Qudsia always had a lump in her throat and all she needed was an excuse to start weeping. Resting her head on the window sill, she shed voluminous tears; seeing a wedding procession always cut her to the quick. But everyone was saddened by this barat.

Was it a barat or a funeral? Life's doors are shut on a young, frail girl, she wants to create a world of dreams and open a small window in it. But the stupid people around her don't allow it because she threatens their beliefs. And what happens? She shatters all their beliefs and turns away from them.

Now Uncle Shabir was neither Krishan Murari nor Ghazi Mian. He was an incomplete, hollow man. He could not turn the snarling vipers in Aunt Qudsia's life into garlands with his flute, nor could he change the cowdung that enveloped her soul into sandalwood by sheer dint of his faith. His total assets were his two trembling hands which he could use well to stifle turbulent emotions. And Aunt Qudsia, at the age of twenty-six, was fading away like a forgotten remark. She didn't even have enough courage to be like Bua and lose her sanity. At least then people would fear her. As things stood now, her Ghazi Mian was ridiculed and pitied. There are those who are more alive in death than the living.

Bua was probably just a few years older than Aunt Qudsia. From the time she is young, a woman's heart is filled with a thousand fears, so that when she reaches puberty she thinks of herself as a fragile, unbaked clay pitcher that must encounter stones at every step. Because she had lost her mind, Bua's fears had vanished, especially her fear of losing her honour. She was no longer a hollow clay pitcher, she was solid rock. In a manly fashion she went where she pleased, regardless of whether it was night or day. Somehow she had managed to make people fear her. Nobody really knew how, but one or two miracles came about and people began to believe. Once a ruffian, finding her alone, tried to grab her. Ghazi Mian slapped his face with such fury that it caved in. At another time an unfortunate fellow tried to force himself on her, and it is believed that the hand which he fastened upon her wrist decomposed and fell off.

Our uncle, Chacha Mian, was an apostate. He used to say, "Every year thousands of lepers throng to the shrine with hopes of being healed. Decomposition of limbs and their subsequent falling off is not a miracle, it's a disease. And it's not unusual for an alcoholic to suffer from an attack of facial paralysis."

But we were afraid of doubting Bua. What would you do if your whole face fell in and collapsed? She had the temperament of an ogress. However, ever since we had discovered that she was not a ghoul or a spirit and was only a little mad, we ceased to be terrified of her.

One day we found her standing under the oak tree, wiping mud from her slipper. I gave her Aunt Qudsia's message.

"I'm not coming," she said rudely. "I'll come when I feel like it." Muttering, she walked away towards the path across the small bridge.

Finally, after a long time, she felt like it and there she was suddenly. Without standing on ceremony, without saying a word to anyone, she went directly to the water pitchers, poured some water in a brass cup for herself and sprinkled some on the chameli buds she had tied in a corner of her dupatta. Then she drew the dupatta over her head, placed her hands on her hips like a nautchi and started smiling. Amma had always warned us that girls from good families don't stand with their hands on their hips, only nautchis do that. While you're growing up there's a time when your hands become a nuisance, you don't know what to do with them. So, driven by the fear that I might become a nautchi if I weren't careful, I would sometimes place both hands over my head.

"What is this, you wretch, why are you slapping your head?" vexed, Amma would scold me.

"Where should I keep my hands then?" I would wearily ask.

"In the fire!" She'd get more irritated. "Get out of here." And I would quickly slip away.

Suddenly Bua laughed. Then she came and sat down on the divan and proceeded to adjust the folds on her tight pajama. Her clothes were clean and spotless. A starched pink dupatta was draped neatly across her shoulders while the bunch of chameli buds tied in a corner swung next to her cheek.

Unable to withstand her stare, Aunt Qudsia lowered her eyes and pretended to busy herself by adjusting her dupatta over her shoulders.

"My eyes are red from weeping…"

She seemed to be teasing Aunt Qudsia.

"Smoking, chewing paan, my beloved/ My cruel beloved didn't come today/My eyes are red from weeping…"

Aunt Qudsia was holding her tears in the palm of her hand; she began sprinkling them. But before she could bring on an attack of hysteria, Bua leapt up and was gone out of the back door in seconds.

Her voice glided in the distance: *"My eyes are red from weeping…"*

Everyone was impressed. Bua had knowledge of hidden things, she knew how to handle Aunt Qudsia.

"She must have heard it from somebody," Chacha Mian said. He was an apostate, you see. But no one paid any attention to his remark. After this episode Bua became a frequent visitor to our house. She'd come, sit down, and if she felt uneasy, she'd just get up and leave.

"Come, stay," Aunt Qudsia cajoled pleadingly.

"No, no I can't…he'll be waiting for me…"

And I'd imagine Ghazi Mian actually standing under the shade of the kadamb tree, waiting for her.

"She's lost her wits, the unfortunate creature, and she's from such a good family, too."

"You know, she doesn't look mad to me."

"Why, you'll think she's mad only after she picks up stones to throw at you? Doesn't she have that low-caste woman in her house, and what does she know of the value of money? Anyone can come in and steal all she's got and she'll never know."

"Don't say anything about her, please, I'm not sure it's safe."

"Why, I'm not saying she's a bad person, am I?"

Once Maulvi Sahib, the village cleric, said to Bua, "You had better get married, girl. What's the good of roaming around like this?"

Enraged, Bua pounced on him: "Why don't *you* get your mother married to some ruffian walking on the streets!"

"A woman is not safe without a man by her side," Maulvi Sahib explained.

Bua exploded: "I have a man by my side, your father's father…if he hears you talk like this he'll set your beard on fire."

Who could chide Ghazi Mian's cherished beloved without incurring his wrath? While returning from the well with a bucket of water, Maulvi Sahib's son was bitten by a snake. Maulvi Sahib's wife fell at Bua's feet, rubbed her nose on her shoes and it was only then that the boy's life was spared.

"It must be a water snake, they're not the poisonous type," Chacha Mian remarked. But who will listen to talk that mocks belief? Fear of Bua grew in people's hearts. She wasn't just anybody, she was Ghazi Mian's most treasured beloved, Ghazi Mian, who made it possible for a barren woman to conceive, who healed a leper, who turned beggars into kings and kings into beggars in seconds. Was it any wonder that he cared so much about his favourite girl?

Since she hadn't produced even a mouse as yet, Aunt Qudsia was sure the mem was barren. Nani Biwi's fasting and prayers had surely put a lock on her fertility. Allah could change everything in no time. Nani Biwi had also made a vow at Mian's shrine that when, with Allah's grace, Qudsia's luck changed and she became pregnant, she would make an offering of a silver figurine.

For three years Nani Biwi's silver cradle had been placed at Mian's feet with the entreaty, "Ghazi Mian, please fill this cradle." And along with that continued the pleas to Qawi Qadir to bring Qudsia's husband back to her. But all the vows, prayers and fasting came to nought. The cradle was filled up, but it was the mem who became the instrument. The day she heard the news that her rival had given birth to a daughter, Aunt Qudsia was weighed down, as if a marble tomb had been erected over her soft, newly-dug grave. On the day of reckoning the angels of death, Munkar and Nakir, would be slow to breathe life into her.

Bua, who had been absent for many days, suddenly appeared. Nani Biwi was busy scolding the nain who had arrived with sweets to offer felicitations on the occasion of the baby's birth. Tossing the ladoos into the gutter, Nani Biwi threatened to shave off the nain's hair; the woman clasped her lahnga about her legs and bolted from there.

On hearing of the arrival of the baby girl, Bua began twittering.

"Listen girl, your soutan's lap has been blessed, aren't you going to distribute sweets?" Then she took down the drum and embarked on silly songs about childbirth.

"*With bells on his ankles/ The little tot will play* cham, cham, cham..."

There was no little tot, what cursed cham, cham was there going to be? This uncalled for singing angered Nani Biwi. She railed and ranted at Bua who dropped the drum, left the house and trudged off to sit behind the mosque. She was gone for many days. This was not unusual. Not caring whether it was night or day, she started off on foot, wandering from one village to another. Somewhere along the way, standing on the edge of a well to catch her breath, if she heard a new song, she'd include it in her repertoire of lyrics. Then she moved on. Often she travelled without food for days. The crazed have great strength. We had never seen her sleeping. She wasn't bothered by either snakes or scorpions or wild animals. In the village on the other side of the stream a lion was spotted, but it stayed out of her path. We had heard rumours that the lion offered her salutations by placing its head on the ground before her.

Bua told her stories of Ghazi Mian's playfulness with such aplomb that it became difficult to doubt her word. When you live next to a shrine everything seems to make sense. Mian was very stubborn and mischievous. He teased her, always tugging at her dupatta or clutching her bangles.

"Now listen, how did he fall in love with you?" Aunt Qudsia asked.

"His heart led him to me," Bua replied, smiling proudly.

"That's what I'm asking, how did his heart lead him to you?" Aunt Qudsia was always anxious to find out how one could win someone's heart. Although she had sacrificed her body, soul and everything she possessed, she had not succeeded in winning anyone's heart.

"I don't know, why don't you ask him yourself, he's standing in front of me, smiling." She pointed to the wall with her finger and all of us followed it fearfully. Our eyes could see nothing, but for her the world around was filled with blinding light.

"How did you meet him?"

"I was on my way to the well, to draw water, he stood in my path blocking my way."

"And then?" We all moved closer to her.

"I tried to run, he clasped my wrist."

"And then?" We edged closer still.

"My father was very amgry." She was in a world of her own already. "He said, we won't give him our daughter, he's a boatman's son."

"A boatman's son?"

Bua explained that Mian had taken the form of a boatman's son in order to beg for her hand; he fell at her father's feet and pleaded. But her father got angry and rejected him, and arranged her marriage to someone else. A terrible storm arose while the wedding party was attempting to cross the Ghagra stream in the middle of the night. It was Mian, transformed as the boatman and oaring their boat, who had summoned the storm. He ignored everyone else and made an attempt to save her from drowning, but the others tried to interfere. Enraged, he tipped the boat and let everyone drown. Surrounded by flowers, Bua floated for three days on the surface of the water in her bridal clothes.

"And then?" We had moved practically into her lap by now.

"And then nothing!" Exhausted, she pushed us away and left the house to wander in the cemetery in a daze, lost, singing love songs.

Bua was a virgin. No man had touched her. After the barat drowned she managed somehow to get to the banks of the stream. For days she strayed in the woods. When her parents heard she was alive they came after her to take her home, but by then Bua had retreated into a world of dreams. She refused to shatter her bridal bangles; she was a bride, and Bale Mian was her bridegroom. No one had the courage to tangle with Bale Mian.

"He's calling me," she'd suddenly say and wander off into the woods, singing songs of love. Considering her desire to be Bale Mian's, no one dared stop her. Gradually, as time passed, certain miracles came to be associated with her and people seemed to be more and more intimidated by her. Then they began to worship her. If someone needed to ask a favour of Mian, she was the one who was pampered first. Wherever she went she was treated with deference, and to have the opportunity of doing something for her was regarded as a stroke of good fortune. When a prayer was answered, a pink dupatta, fragrant oil and attar, bangles and flowers were offered at Ghazi Mian's shrine for her, along with the offering that had been promised for Ghazi Mian. How much did she eat? She could stay without food for days. People filled large decorated trays with food and brought them to her house and she distributed the food among beggars. She had been living alone since the death of her parents. A low-caste woman took care of the house. The village washer-woman, who was careless with everyone else's clothes and frequently lost or misplaced laundry, washed Bua's clothes with the utmost care, giving them the best crispness and lustre. Bua owned some land, but never bothered to make any profit from its tilling. Perhaps that was why people had begun to view her as Ghazi Mian's cherished beloved, there were hundreds who were ready to surrender their lives to her. Therefore, although she was a weak woman, she was not handicapped or helpless; she claimed all the rights of a man. She moved about alone, as she fancied, declared her love in a loud voice, sang boisterously, made bold comments without reserve, swore unabashedly, sat in the company of men while a qawwali was going on and generously threw money to the singers.

During the annual fair at Ghazi Mian's shrine, thousands of ruffians and scoundrels trooped in along with the lakhs of pilgrims and worshippers; every other day you heard about kidnappings and rapes. Upper class women considered it dangerous to come out even in enclosed palanquins or guarded carriages. And Bua, all the while, sailed about without a care among the crowds, her dupatta floating behind her.

"My word, Bua, the world is a dangerous place, don't go to the fair," Amma warned her. "Aren't you afraid to wander around all by yourself?"

"But I don't wander by myself. I'm not alone, he's with me." In other words, her *he*.

There was no one among us who could contradict her. What could you say? And if we said something she didn't like we'd be in trouble; who knows what miracle might follow.

"She's a degenerate, the wretch!" In the beginning Chacha Mian didn't like her at all. "And she's not mad, either. She's just making a fool of all of us."

That very night Chacha Mian suffered an attack of liver pain that left him gasping for breath. He kept insisting that he'd had a liver ailment for many years, but who was going to pay any attention to what he said? "He's an ignorant man," Amma admitted to Bua in an attempt to win her over. She secretly begged her to speak to Ghazi Mian on their behalf.

The pain would have subsided on its own, but Amma was sure he had been cured because of Bua's intervention. And she warned Chacha Mian that if he ever said another unfavourable word concerning Bua again, she would beat her head with her hands. What did he have to lose? He had no children and no God, while she, by God's grace, was a mother and could not afford to antagonise anyone. As for Abba, she had already sworn that if he said anything hostile with regard to Bua he would surely see her dead. Abba had often maintained that this business of believing in spiritual leaders and their followers was a sinful undertaking. But Amma's family was dearer to her than concerns about the next life.

When our friendship with Bua grew it seemed as if we'd come to terms with God; because of Bua we felt as if we too had some connection with Ghazi Mian. Sometimes, when she was in a good mood, she spent the night at our house and all of us quarrelled for the opportunity to sleep with her on the same bed. She exuded a wonderful fragrance of soft-smelling, freshly-dug earth. When, after several days of absence, her voice floating in song reached our ears, we became frantic with excitement and ran to fetch her. Like ants we clung to her, dragging her home. The very same voice which used to strike fear in our hearts now fell on our ears with the magic of an ancient melody.

As soon as she stepped into the house, everything brightened and came to life, the drum beat vibrated:

"Ho, my raja, bring me some medicine from Dilli/ So I can be cured."
She sang the new songs and new tunes she had picked up.
"The rains are here/My brother, will you not put up the swing?"

Dark clouds swirled, raindrops fell, young hearts stirred with emotions, flames smouldered in Aunt Qudsia's eyes. Who was going to put up a swing? Aunt Qudsia became dizzy and nauseous when she saw anyone swinging. But Bua brought a length of rope from somewhere, we made a swing, and with a down pillow for a seat we swung high and low. Bua sang long, high notes and Aunt Qudsia, from her place on the divan, joined in:

"My heart yearns, the clouds pour/ My friend, how will I endure these days of spring..."

Sitting at a distance Uncle Shabir stared at the floor like a criminal, as though he had a hand in making the clouds pour and the heart yearn, as if Aunt Qudsia's spring had soured because of him. Qudsia belonged to someone else, she was forbidden fruit. Secretly he consulted maulvis, talked to lawyers, but we're talking of the time when the Khul's Bill hadn't been passed. At first no one thought of divorce because of the fear of bringing dishonour to the family. Then, after some of the rebels in the family succeeded in bringing Nani Biwi around to the idea, Aunt Qudsia's husband stubbornly refused to give in.

Rejecting our world, Bua had created a free world of her own where she ruled. She had sealed all doors but after all she was a woman; a chink remained somewhere. We became very fond of her and sometimes affectionately made obstinate demands; when she got ready to leave we trailed her tearfully, forcing her to turn back.

"Bua, these silly children are crazy about you, why don't you take them with you," Amma would say, and Bua would cancel her trip.

If she hadn't been slightly demented, Bua was fit to be weighed in gold. She had started helping out with chores in the house. Cleaning was her particular obsession. Accompanied by an army of kids she went about tidying up and threw out basketfuls of rubbish. If only she could come back with us to our hometown after Abba's retirement.

"Can't she be cured?" Amma asked Hakim Sahib who used to be called in to treat Aunt Qudsia. He came to our house once or twice every week.

"Of course she can, Begum Sahib. There is no ailment in this world for which medicine doesn't have a cure. Start giving her a laxative and God willing, her mind will return to its normal state."

Hakim Sahib had only one medicine for every ailment: laburnum purgative. When Aunt Qudsia felt unwell, it was this very laxative that was administered to her. Not only did you feel that your life was slipping away but your body also seemed to be threatened by the effects of these laxatives. She had no recourse but to be cured, and for days afterwards she was afraid to blink for fear that it might be mistaken for an oncoming attack. Chacha Mian, too, had been given these laxatives for the pain in his liver. After the first dose he threatened to kill Hakim Sahib.

"The heat from the body travels to the brain. Purging the stomach helps get rid of all noxious matter." Hakim Sahib proceeded to throw light on the advantages of purgative therapy and everyone was convinced. Bua, however, ignored his advice.

"Come now, what's this silly hakim going to do for me." Irritated by all this talk, Bua made off. No one could discuss her illness for any length of time.

It was while a treatment for Bua was being sought that something tragic occurred, which clearly confirmed her unbalanced state of mind. One of our cousins, the third among her siblings, was rather homely and the family faced constant hurdles in finding her a suitable match. After much hard work an aunt from Saharanpur finally got something going. The boy's mother arrived to talk things over. The house was cleaned so thoroughly to impress her that we began to feel like guests in our own home. Displayed all around us were items which we had never been allowed near for fear that we might break or tarnish them.

Bua had not made an appearance for many days. After a frantic search lasting three or four days, we gave up on her. A lengthy menu was being prepared for the mother-in-law, the samdhan. Suddenly, chameli buds dangling from a corner of her dupatta, a new song on her lips, Bua arrived in her usual way. First, she was taken aback by the manner in which the house had been cleaned and decorated.

Then she spotted the guest and lost control altogether. Going up to the woman, Bua flicked her eyelashes and knit her brows as if searching for a microscopic tic. The samdhan was not invisible. True, she was short, but her lack of height was amply made up for by her massive bulk.

Amma was perturbed by Bua's behaviour and made an attempt to distract her with some silly chatter. But, pushing aside Amma's restraining hand, Bua asked the samdhan-to-be: "I say, sister, what kind of grain do you eat?"

The samdhan's face came alive with a variety of emotions. The diamond nose-pin vibrated in the smooth, black nose and it seemed as if she was about to explode with a loud bang.

"Bua dear, will you take this ice-water to the men's quarters?" Amma pulled her away from their guest. "Number Three has received a proposal, why don't you go and see the groom and tell us what he's like—he's outside." Amma managed to get her to leave.

"She's mad, the wretch," Amma apologised.

But the samdhan would not be appeased.

Bua left the room and returned within seconds. Dumping the tray with the ice-water on the divan, she beat her forehead with her hand.

"O my mother! Is that a groom or a tobacco leaf and a dwarf to boot!" She placed her right hand over her left, fingers extended, thumb to thumb to show them what she meant.

Bua continued: "I tell you, they don't make a proper pair. The groom is no good, you'll only ruin the girl's life. I say samdhan, go and find someone who's a fairy like yourself for your son, and leave our girl alone."

The samdhan didn't explode, but she did leave Number Three alone.

Vexed, Bua kept swearing; Amma could not calm her down. Taking the drum down from the peg she began a song on a high note:

A dark lover I won't take, sister, a dark lover...

When my groom sits beside me on the nuptial bed, I'll kick him so he falls, sister.

A dark lover... I won't take."

Poor Number Three was fated to live with hurdles. The whole household reprimanded Bua for her actions, but thrusting the drum to one side, she continued to mutter: "Is she unwanted baggage, hunh?"

She was gone for many weeks this time. We thought she wasn't coming back. The house was lonely without her and Aunt Qudsia's attacks recurred with greater frequency. Her temperament also soured. In the past she had complied with everything Nani Biwi said.

"Qudsia, child, drink some milk."

"Yes, Bi Amma."

"Child, lie down, give your back a rest, you've been stretched like a rod all day."

"Girl, how long are you going to remain in bed, get up now."

In other words it was always "Get up," "Eat this, drink that." Like a disease, Aunt Qudsia was affixed to Nani Biwi who constantly expressed her grief at her daughter's fate and continuously scrutinised her. What else was there for her to do, anyway? And Aunt Qudsia answered with, "Yes, Bi Amma," to everything.

Suddenly, no one knows why, Aunt Qudsia began to get irritated with Nani Biwi. The two would quarrel with each other, sometimes Aunt Qudsia would cry and sometimes Nani Biwi. And Dadima invariably jumped in. One by one all the aunts in the house would also be embroiled in the battle and before long two separate parties emerged. It all started with one thing and ended somewhere else altogether.

Members from our mother's side of the family formed one group while those from our father's side formed another. Attacks directed at seven generations of each party commenced. And later, their faces swollen, all the women stiffly avoided each other for days.

Every skirmish originated from Aunt Qudsia's camp. The bitterness in her temperament grew with each passing day; she seemed to derive pleasure from hurting those around her. Her behaviour towards Uncle Shabir also became chilly.

"*Why, when I called for you, did you take so long?*" he began with one of Aunt Qudsia's favourite pieces. She turned her back to him. The poor fellow squirmed uncomfortably.

"You should go, it's getting dark and it's the rainy season," she said dryly, feeling sorry for him. Grateful that she was thinking of him at least, he got up and left.

And then one day we went mad with joy. We found her. It was spring, the woods were blazing with palash blossoms, our eyes seemed to be brimming over with the red of the flowers. She was standing next to an amber-laden tree, dusting sand from her slippers. Her pink dupatta glowed from the fiery reflection of the flowers, spring blossoms danced in her eyes as if she had just come from a visit with her beloved or was on her way to meet him.

"Wait, wait a minute, I'm coming." We dragged her. Suddenly she paused, cast a glance behind her and said in a pleading tone, "I'll be back soon."

We were nonplussed. To whom was she making a promise of return? There was no one there. She took a few steps, then stopped. Angrily she said, "Don't put on an act with me, I'm warning you!" Then she made as if to walk on. Once again, as if she had heard some objectionable remark, she knit her brow and scolded: "All right, you can go, I won't come back... I'll see what you'll do...you don't trust me... I don't care..." She was fighting the air and our legs seemed to be melting. If we hadn't loved her so much we would have made off from there a long time ago.

Bua's arrival caused a stir in our house. It was a strange coincidence that whenever she came, a parcel containing fruit or sweetmeats arrived or we received some good news. Her appearance livened everyone's hearts; if a fight was in progress, it ceased, or maybe in the ensuing commotion people forgot what they had been fighting about. Shrugging off her despondency, Aunt Qudsia also got up and took note of what was going on.

"I'm not coming," Bua scolded the air in front of her. Everyone became fearful.

"What's the matter?" Amma asked.

"Such grief. He's pestering me, he doesn't trust me, he says I have another lover, I have eyes for someone else!" She screamed as she complained about Bale Mian. "Who does he think I am…a hussy?" "Ahhh…you crazy girl," Amma said sadly and sighed again.

"He's burnt to a cinder with jealousy, he says I'm fickle!" Her imaginary lover was an odd composite indeed; a little bit of James Bond, a little of Krishan Murari, you might say. James Bond is a hero for every age, whether he appears as a hero from *Dastan-e-Amir Hamza* or as Hatim Tai. And her beloved was also a reflection of Krishan Murari because people generally sang songs about Krishan. As a matter of fact, Bale Mian's antics reminded you of him: tugging at her dupatta, twisting her wrists so that her bangles broke, and when moved to anger, resorting to slapping or upturning a boat.

He exhibited all the traits of a suave young man. No matter what anyone might say, Bua's Bale Mian was undoubtedly more colourful and vibrant than Aunt Qudsia's Uncle Shabir. We believed everything Bua told us. Why was it so surprising that she could see Bale Mian? Didn't we observe elephants and stallions in the clouds, and Raja Inder's court in all its glory in the peeling plaster of the crumbling, saline-ridden walls? We didn't think she was deranged. If there were a few deranged people like her in every household, life would certainly be more tolerable.

"I say Bua, won't you come here for a minute," Amma cajoled; she had something to say to her that was important. Perhaps because Bua was angry with Mian, she didn't bolt when Amma brought up the question of Hakim Sahib's treatment. It seemed that she was listening intently.

"Ahhh…what treatment…my suffering at his hands will take my life…he grumbles at every step, then he tyrannises…me.

Taking the drum from its hook she gazed at it ruefully.

"Little mouse, why do you gather all this treasure/ Soon all will be taken away…"

When the drum failed to perk her up she began quarrelling with Bale Mian:

"Beloved, your tantrums I won't tolerate anymore…
I tell you, if you climb a horse, I'll climb an elephant…

Beloved, your tantrums…"

She wore her beloved out. If he climbed the roof, she climbed a mountain, if he followed her to the mountain, she darted into the infernal regions under the earth; in other words, she made him huff and puff.

"Look, here he is, touching my feet, begging forgiveness."

The insane are like kings in their own realm. What confidence Bua had in herself. The king of kings bowed at her feet, one smile from her and he was no longer himself. If you can find someone who cares for you like this why should you not discard the life of reason and good sense?

When birds who are caged gaze at the flight of those soaring freely in the skies, they are bound to dash their heads against the wooden bars of their cages. And, unable to find escape, they conspire with their captors. Isn't it true that domesticated fowls or birds with clipped wings are used by hunters to ensnare their own kind?

The good women enclosed in the four walls of their homes, tightly bound by the constraints of society, also could not tolerate Bua's freedom. She was a woman, but she enjoyed the rights of men and everyone resented that. Bua didn't refuse to take the laxative, but she also didn't protest strongly.

Amma said that the wretch's yes or no was all the same; after all, the treatment was for her own good.

All night long amaltas pods, amla, har, bahir and other items from the same disgusting family continued to be emptied into a large, unpolished copper pot. After her morning prayers Nani Biwi raised the heat under the pot again. Bua had been detained under some pretext.

The first dose had to be taken on an empty stomach, first thing in the morning. We also awoke. The whole house was putrid with the smell of amaltas. The sight of the large tin bowl filled with a mixture that looked like rotting cow-dung, made my stomach turn.

Bua tried to shake her off, but Amma pressed on with pledges on her own life. Nani Biwi pleaded on Mian's behalf. They brought her to the edge of the water drain and told her to squat.

"Hold your nose with your dupatta," Dadi Amma suggested.

The entire family had gathered as if a fighting match between rams was about to commence. Bua pressed her nose with her dupatta and with Tai Amma's help she balanced the large bowl with one hand.

"Don't make her drink this... Amma Bi... O God, Apa Bi, leave the poor wretch alone." Suddenly Aunt Qudsia was pleading with everybody. "Please, you're so nice, Tai Amma..."

She had suffered the tortures of this laxative.

"My word, girl, are you out of your mind!"

"Alakh! Alakh!" We made gagging noises as we sat close by with our noses pressed between our fingers.

"No, Apa Bi...please, don't make her drink this. I've had it, may God help us!"

"Because you've had it you're still in one piece. You might have been picking at straws by now if you hadn't."

With great ceremony Bua took one sip from the cup and "phurr!" she spat it all out on Tai Amma's breast. Throwing the bowl into the drain, she made a beeline for the tap and gargled until she was spent.

"May he die, that bastard hakim, it's his mother's crushed liver in this drink."

Each time she washed out her mouth she delivered a solid invective intended for Hakim Sahib. "May his mother's grave be filled with worms!"

"You foolish girl, you've dumped such valuable medicine into the gutter. If you didn't want it you should have said so in the beginning, we could have saved it for Qudsia."

Aunt Qudsia winced.

"I didn't throw it, he pushed it out of my hand." Placing the blame on Bale Mian, Bua calmly began chewing cardamom seeds.

"But he was not talking to you," Tai Amma said irately.

"Oh, he is such a vagabond! Who can fight him? Last night he wouldn't leave me alone, he clasped my feet, begged forgiveness and cried."

May God forgive us!

Bua rose nonchalantly and got ready to leave. "Why, where are you off to?"

"I have to go, he's getting angry with me again. *Beloved, I'll be a chameli in your lap...*" She was one with her beloved once more.

A travelling theatre was in town, we were all longing to go. Bua went without a ticket every day and picked up new songs of burning love.

Aunt Qudsia's behaviour was changing. Instead of reading Rashid-ul-Kheri's *The Morning of Sorrow* and *The Night of Life* and sobbing, she now surreptitiously read *The Poems of Love's Poison*, and at night she paced the courtyard.

"Sir, the wretch will absolutely not take the laxative," Amma complained to Hakim Sahib.

"No matter. By Allah's grace, I have other drugs, she will never guess she is taking anything. Here, give her these three tablets rolled in paan or some sweets. Continue this treatment once every three days and, God willing, she will be completely cured."

"Here, Bua, have a paan." As soon as Bua appeared Amma would open her paandan.

"No dear, no, my breath will smell." Bua dodged Amma adroitly.

But if women don't have anything better to do than meddle, how long can you escape from them? Perhaps she had a quarrel with Bale Mian or maybe his attention strayed, but somehow the first dose finally went down Bua's throat. And everyone waited for the results. Nothing happened. Except that Bua placed a rope cot under the neem tree and went to sleep, something we had never seen her do before.

Everyone was convinced that Bale Mian had played a trick by impeding the progress of the tablet, or possibly it hadn't been administered first thing in the morning and that was why no results were in evidence. Suddenly Bua awoke with a start. For the first time we saw a strange expression of undefined fear on her face. She undoubtedly had knowledge of the unknown. She got up and left angrily.

"I say, to hell with this wretched treatment! What if she leaves a curse or two behind, where will we be? One shouldn't tangle with the pious." Amma made her decision.

"It is truly amazing, the tablet had no effect on her," impressed, Nani Biwi proclaimed.

But in the evening surprise fell upon us like a mud slide. Bua's sweepress came running to our house with the message that Bua had been suffering from dysentery all morning and now she was also vomiting. Bewildered, Amma sent off a servant to Hakim Sahib.

"It's the heat flowing out," Hakim Sahib remarked, and handed the servant a potion which reduced the flow of the heat, but caused Bua's temperature to rise at an alarming rate.

Amma sent for her several days in a row, but she refused to come. She hardly ate much earlier and now her sweepress came and fetched some watery rice and khichri and sago pudding, but Bua didn't touch a thing. All she did was drink large quantities of water.

When she came after several weeks, we felt as if she was distanced from us, as if we had remained children while she had matured. When we tried to put our arms around her neck she tottered and sat down.

"Come now, what silliness is this." She spoke in a brusque tone, as though we had never draped our arms around her neck like a garland before this. Her clothes were rumpled, her hair dry and bedraggled. She had always been thin, now, after the illness, she was worse. When we requested her to play the drum she hedged. Amma placed a tray of pea-pods before her. She started shelling them.

Nani Biwi and Amma exchanged meaningful glances above her head. They both expressed relief; if the remaining two tablets could also be administered, no signs of the illness would remain.

"I say, Bua, Mian isn't upset with you, is he?" Amma probed.

"Am I the one to fight?" This meant that a dispute was in progress. "I don't know what he thinks of himself, that son of a lat sahib!" She seemed perturbed. There was, without a doubt, a falling-out between them.

Bua's sweepress had gone to a neighbouring village to perform an abortion. Her usual trade was rolling twine, but occasionally, as a side business, she helped the needy. Amma persuaded Bua to spend the night at our house.

Amma was ready to swear on the Quran that she had not given Bua the second dose, but Dadi Amma insisted that she and Nani Biwi had been conspiring; the second dose had been given and had acted like an acid bomb. Bua collapsed from a wave of diarrhoea that seemed to have no end. That night things became so bad that Abba also got wind of what was going on. The doctor was sent for, he prescribed medication, but Bua suffered helplessly from loose motions all night long.

Abba thundered that the Hakim Sahib ought to be whipped, he was a fool, and that if he prescribed any medicine for anyone again he would be handcuffed.

Dadi Amma had been kept out of all this good work. It was Nani Biwi's special case and she wanted to man her position herself.

"I say, girls, what is going on?" Dadi Amma, who was quite deaf, would occasionally repeat this question.

"Nothing, sister dear…mind your own business!" Nani Biwi uttered the first part of the sentence loudly and the second almost inaudibly.

"Nobody tells me anything," Dadi Amma muttered. The two were always at odds with each other. They were samdhans, but were also sisters-in-law by marriage. However, the real reason for their dissent lay in the fact of their beliefs. Nani Biwi belonged to the Sunni sect while Dadi Amma was a Shia. Their cantonments were set up in the different verandas. Amma came and sat in Nani Biwi's veranda early in the morning. Amma was the nucleus around whom our household revolved; it is obvious that her veranda assumed greater importance. After offering salutations to Dadi Amma, Amma came and sat down. The door to Aunt Qudsia's room also opened on this veranda, Aunt Qudsia, who was the family's most urgent social issue. Her comings and goings caused the place to bustle. Uncle Shabir too sat there. And as for the children, they will be where all the activity is. Dadi Amma was jealous: because the children's paternal side of the family was Shia, they should be raised as Shia as well. However, Nani Biwi had all the power; at every step she praised the tenets of the Sunni sect.

We were backed by Amma. When we didn't heed Dadi Amma's injunctions, Amma reprimanded us with a smile and we were emboldened. But if we ignored Nani Biwi's orders, we had to listen to threats of bones being shattered.

Both sides attempted to show us the straight road leading to heaven. Dadi Amma taught us one kalima, while Nani Biwi taught us the other. Confused, we jumbled them up, something that had an effect on us similar to that of Hakim Sahib's tablets, we felt as if we had taken a mental purgative. The keys to heaven got all mixed up and both sides showered us with damnation.

Nani Biwi held milad in answer to Dadi Amma's majalis; we got fine-grained sweets in earthen cups and immediately became Sunnis. But when the coverings were removed from the chandeliers in Dadi Amma's veranda and the taboot was brought out, we became hers completely; when nobas were recited in tremulous voices we donned black shirts and beat our chests with vigour. Nani Biwi pummelled us and tempted us with colourful sweets, but it was wise to be a member of Dadi Amma's party during the holy month of Muharram. For us the doors to heaven opened on the side where goods were most plentiful.

"Girl, are you Sunni or Shia?" Dadi Amma would frequently ask.

"Shia," I would reply promptly.

"Are you Shia or Sunni?" Nani Biwi usually queried before handing out sweets. Thank God the two verandas were at some distance from each other and both grandmothers were somewhat hard of hearing.

The question of Bua's treatment took a rather unpleasant turn. Dadi Amma filled Abba's ears with gossip, he scolded Amma, Amma cried heartily.

Abba's retirement was approaching. Prosperity makes you large-hearted and you feel great affection for your relatives. But with the onset of hard times, the fountains of love also dry up. All his life Abba had spent money indiscriminately. Now, with only a few years left before retirement, he wanted to make up for all that careless spending.

Everyone stiffened when a crow cawed. Here comes another guest. The crow cawed at our house every day; when our relatives from our father's side poured in, our mother's relatives, not wishing to be left behind, arrived as well. If paternal aunts showed up with their spouses and children, then maternal aunts also made an appearance with their entire families in tow.

The guests fell into two camps. Two tables were set up and spies were sent out to make sure that the opposing camp was not receiving preferential treatment. Usually Nani Biwi's party had the upper hand since Amma was in her camp.

Abba had no time for party politics. In addition, he was the one who made the money and Amma the one who spent it. The situation was very similar to what it's like in America these days; everyone, regardless of which party each person belonged to, pampered her. Abba, on the other hand, was neutral. He treated both parties in the same way.

However, Chacha Mian, my father's younger brother, was the one who was always looking for an opportunity to make trouble between the two parties.

Amma entertained her in-laws well, but in a way that reeked openly of disaffection. If there was a shortage of food she would announce the fact in a loud voice: "Send it over there, we'll eat with chutney and pickle."

But Chacha Mian was a sly one; he ate with Amma's party, partaking of whatever special dish it was that had proven unplentiful, and then went over to Dadi Amma's camp and said, "The liver and kidneys cooked today were excellent." There were no liver and kidneys cooked that day.

Dadi Amma grumbled: "My word, I've had a hankering for so many days; no one bothered to send us any, they wolfed it all down themselves!"

And the following day when Abba came from court and went to greet her, she immediately complained about the liver and kidneys. Abba said to Amma, "I say, why didn't you send some liver and kidneys over there?"

"My word! When did we have liver and kidneys?" Amma would stand up in a huff.

"I swear, I saw it with my own eyes, Bakreedan took over a bowlful," Dadi Amma declared, relying on Chacha Mian's word. Oaths would be taken, faiths dragged in, and finally Chacha Mian would be called. He would say innocently, "What liver and kidneys? I've said so many times we shouldn't eat watermelon with rice, now I have a pain in my kidneys and once the pain starts…" Chacha Mian tried to change the subject.

"Did you eat liver and kidneys over there or not?" Dadi Amma persisted.

"When? I didn't get any. This is not fair, such rich foods being cooked and eaten by others."

No one really knew what was going on. Witnesses were brought forth, then someone who was feeling heavy-hearted burst into tears, in answer to which another person broke down; old wounds were rubbed anew.

"All I did was ask for a tiny morsel and she was downright evasive…"

"Such a blow it was, the fingers left a mark on the poor wretch's face."

"I say, sister, it's quite another matter when it comes to your own kin…"

"Yes, indeed, and we're just enemies…"

When all of them were exhausted, Chacha Mian stepped in.

"What's all this bickering? You sound like butchers and common people…what kind of decency is this…fighting over morsels like dogs."

Hearing him scold, everyone, exhausted and worn out by now, felt contrite and went off to bed. Members of the paternal side of the family were glad that Nani Biwi's party had been severely reproached on account of Bua.

Bua was very sick. The time for the third dose never came; she was no good to herself after the second. If Qais had been administered all three doses prescribed by Hakim Sahib he would never have become

Majnun, the crazed lover. He would have lost the vigour needed to roam the desert and the energy to cry out "Laila! Laila!" The poor fellow would have forgotten all about love's sprightliness.

The fever subsided, but for several days afterwards Bua was so weak she could barely talk. Because the second dose had produced immediate results, she was still at our house.

All day long she sat silently in a corner, her eyes shut. Her reason had made a comeback; she seemed quite sensible now.

Bua's sweepress had not yet returned. Amma pampered Bua to no end and personally prepared soup for her. But Bua, her face drawn, would not budge. After much coaxing she would take a few sips but immediately throw up; either that, or she had to set up her cot next to the toilet. Her digestive system was permanently damaged; heat seemed to flow out without the aid of medicine.

Where has Bua gone, I wondered sometimes. That jaunty, proud Bua who ran about with the children shaking the branches of the jambolana tree for jamuns, our mad Bua who stole melons and cucumbers from the fields! Why did Allah give her back her reason? She had even forgotten to laugh.

And singing?

After the second dose her throat became hoarse.

O God, she'll never again put up a swing on the neem tree and sing songs about the rainy season.

Amma had appointed herself Bua's guardian. She arranged to have her house rented and Bua began to live with us. When the sweepress returned, she came to Bua distraught. Bua's health was relatively better at this time. She was peeling potatoes for potato bharta. Because winter had begun, she spent most of her time in the kitchen.

There was a time when, during the coldest winter months, Bua went around with just a light shawl draped over her shoulders at night. But that was when she had been filled with warmth.

Amma scolded the sweepress and sent her off. Bua continued to sit quietly with her head lowered. As soon as the rent from the house started coming in, Amma put it all together and ordered a pair of gold bracelets for Bua. When the bracelets, decorated with carved lion heads, arrived, Bua turned them over a few times in her hands, then handed them to Amma.

"Keep them."

"I say, girl, put them on," Nani Biwi insisted.

"My word, no, what's the occasion for wearing bracelets?" she replied tartly. Bua had also developed the ability to tell the difference between what was proper and what was not.

"Do you see her? Who can say the poor girl was once mad. How mature she is now." Nani Biwi called her dullness, maturity.

Bua didn't mention Bale Mian either. If one of us asked, "Bua, how is Mian?" she pretended he had been nothing to her, as if he were a stranger. We teased her further.

"Don't chew my brains!" she'd snap at us and Amma would censure us and shoo us away.

"I say, don't remind her, the wretch, she'll lose her mind again." Nani Biwi also scolded, but she too teased Bua sometimes.

"I say, it seems your Ghazi Mian has forgotten you altogether."

Bua sat still as if she were deaf.

But one day she showed some of her old spirit.

If she watched her diet carefully she was able to keep everything down. By now she had taken over most of the housework and had graduated from light jobs to frying garlic in ghee and pouring it over the dal. Every day she kneaded five seers of dough and before long she was also cooking rotis.

"He's unfaithful," Bua said archly. Then she became emotional. She had been drying her hair after a bath. She looked a little like the Bua of old. Suddenly she broke into songs in a lifeless voice:

"Ho, raja ji, my rival has long tresses / Don't get caught, raja ji…"

The old passion was gone from her voice. Bale Mian had been unfaithful to her or was about to be. Seeing her own dry hair she was suddenly threatened by her rival's long tresses.

"Ho, raja ji…my rival has pink cheeks…"

Bua's once wheatish complexion had become muddy and lustreless. All of a sudden she was stooping like an old woman. When she got to her feet she braced herself by putting both hands on her knees. The old vitality and sprightliness had disappeared; after forsaking Bale Mian's love, she was dispossessed and vacant, a ruin.

~

Childhood never mourns any loss for long. We moved on, leaving her behind as she lagged. Aunt Qudsia was no longer the same either. Instead of constantly complaining about the noise we made, she now called us to her and resolved our disputes, tutored us, scrubbed our dry, chapped hands and feet and massaged them with Vaseline. It wasn't long ago that she had wandered listless and morose, her hair uncombed for many days, her clothes filthy because she would forget to change. Why would a woman adorn herself if the person whose gaze matters the most turns away from her? However, in consideration of her married state she continued wearing two glass bangles on each wrist. People recounted tales of her patience and loyalty with awe and wonder.

A soft, delicate change had begun to appear in her. Instead of staying in bed for hours she started walking regularly. Her complexion blossomed, perhaps because she used a turmeric paste prepared from a fine selection of herbs. In the past when Nani Biwi combed her hair, big clumps would fall out. Now her hair was silky and shiny, probably because it was washed with shika kai, nagar motha and other fragrant roots that are generally used by brides. Or maybe we now liked everything about her because she no longer considered us a curse from God, but thought of us instead as mischievious children.

In the past she carelessly dipped her dupattas in any odd shade of purple or yellow dye (in deference to her wedded state), and threw them out to dry on the line. Now, ever since she had sent for the bale of muslin # 26 from Agra, the dupattas were dyed in soft, sober colours. First the clothes were tailored to match the season, and then matching gold or silver lace was stitched on to the dupattas. For Muharram the colour was green, and for spring they were dyed in five-toned, wavy stripes. We happily transported bucketfuls of water to her, flung her gold-embroidered dupatta up and down, this way and that in the sun to dry, and dumped heaps of half-opened buds next to her pillow.

We looped her earrings with clusters of buds, wrapped the earrings in moist cloth and left them by the water containers. In the evening she bathed, donned a soft-hued, crisp gharara along with an embroidered muslin shirt, with which she wore a gathered dupatta, put on the earrings laden with flowers, and smilingly gazed into the empty air before her as if she too had a Ghazi Mian standing there, teasing her.

The responsible women in the household were a little concerned about the changes they saw in Aunt Qudsia. The attacks of hysteria she had suffered from were understandable; every unfortunate woman who is rejected by her husband occupies herself thus. But dressing up and wearing flowers does not become a woman whose earthly God has turned away from her. She must thank God for whatever meagre clothing she can obtain, cover herself with it, and eat whatever little comes her way. What would people say if they got a glimpse of her fanciful behaviour?

Surely she would be spat at.

All this adornment, these rosettes, they enflame wicked thoughts, the devil gets encouragement from them.

"I say, Qudsia, you don't look well, should I send for Hakim Sahib?" Nani Biwi, fearful of her daughter's well-being, suggested.

"No, Amma Bi, I'm feeling fine." Aunt Qudsia guiltily evaded her mother's gaze.

"My word, sleeping late again! Why, you've missed your morning prayers, girl!"

"I've said the make-up prayers, Amma."

"God knows what rubbish you read all night. Is it any wonder you can't get up in time for morning prayers?"

Every other day Aunt Qudsia received a fresh batch of novels in the mail. Not once did she show them to anyone. As soon as a fresh shipment arrived, she immediately hid it under her pillow.

These days when Aunt Qudsia wore earrings or bangles, Nani Biwi reacted with indignation: "What's the occasion for these earrings?" she'd ask.

"No occasion, I just felt like wearing them," Aunt Qudsia would reply, tossing her head, making the earrings swing.

"My, oh my, what feeling is this?" Nani Biwi grumbled.

There was a time when Nani Biwi had mourned, expressing sorrow at the sight of Aunt Qudsia's unadorned wrists, lamenting that she couldn't wear earrings. "Ahhh, what hopes went into all this jewellery...the poor girl wasn't destined to use any of it. I say, Qudsia, put on a thing or two at Eid or Baqr-Eid at least."

"Who shall I wear it for, Amma?" Aunt Qudsia would respond with a deep sigh.

But all that was in the past. And now? No, the signs were not at all good; reading those wretched, cheap books all night long, pacing the veranda and sighing, looking up at the sky and smiling to oneself...no, these are not the ways of girls who sacrifice their lives for the family. Why were buds sprouting from this old, dried-out trunk?

No longer did Nani Biwi pray with the same zeal for Aunt Qudsia's husband's return. The groom didn't show his face, but Uncle Shabir, on the other hand, came regularly. He seemed to be getting taller with each passing day; he gave the impression that, like a juggler, he had stilts attached to his legs.

Assuming an air of indifference, he would come and sit down at some distance. Aunt Qudsia nonchalantly played with her dupatta which kept slipping from her shoulders, and the gold buttons, in the meantime, became heavier and sank deeper into her chest. Those two didn't need to use their eyes to gaze at each other.

Soon she'd prompt one of us to ask Uncle Shabir to sing *"Sarkar Madine-walle."* We preferred *"The eyes spoke/ plunging a dagger into the heart."* However, in order to make Aunt Qudsia happy we would pester Uncle Shabir to sing the *na'at*.

"Let him sit on the stool here," she would say encouragingly, and we brought him over to the stool.

He would start singing and if, impelled by boredom, we tried to slip away, Aunt Qudsia caught hold of us and, whispering promises of carrot halva and laddus in our ears, made us stay. It was as if she were guilty and could not be left alone with him. Our presence gave them an opportunity to say God knows what to each other; we never understood much. Often, Aunt Qudsia suddenly broke into a laugh for no apparent reason and continued laughing. We too joined in; children don't always have to know why they're laughing. Auntie's complexion glowed and the flower-laden earrings swayed and kissed her cheeks. With everyone laughing, Uncle Shabir's eyes also brimmed with light and his wooden mouth came to life.

"You're laughing for no reason, you silly girl!" he'd say ever so softly. But Auntie heard him.

"So, do you want me to weep all my life?"

"No, Qudsia! I... I want..." he fumbled.

"Whom do you want?" Aunt Qudsia interjected, twisting his words to suit her meaning.

"Qudsia..." Mumble, murmur...whatever he said was unintelligible to us.

We stared at them like idiots.

Mumble, murmur... Aunt Qudsia was saying something. We didn't know what they were saying to each other. But we were aware that a delightfully sweet conversation was in progress. The expressions on their faces filled us with joy; children often understand unspoken words, feel them. We giggled loudly and they used our laughter as a screen behind which to hide.

"Liar! Swear on my life!"

"But how can I swear on *my* life?" he would reply so softly that stone-deaf Nani Biwi could not hear a thing. Dadi Amma's encampment was some distance away.

The two parties were embroiled in battle these days. Dadi Amma sent over some sweetmeats.

"It must be impure."

Nani Biwi maintained that Shias spat into food before handing it out to others or else mixed excrement with it. She threw the grainy, sugar-sweet laddus to the ducks in front of everyone, leaving Dadi Amma fuming with anger. But when Nani Biwi sent her some loquat that had arrived from Saharanpur, Dadi Amma immediately handed the fruit over to her sweepress.

"Be sure to wash them," she said loudly to her, hoping to rile Nani Biwi.

Anyway, Aunt Qudsia would say something and the atmosphere would become taut. She insisted on forcing Uncle Shabir to look into her eyes. However, he avoided her, pinning his gaze instead on the bricks on the floor with an intensity that made one think that, if he looked away, the bricks would jump up and run from there.

When it was evening Uncle Shabir left, but lights continued to glimmer in Aunt Qudsia's eyes, and the smile that played on her lips was reminiscent of the cocky one that hovered on Bua's lips when she saw Bale Mian. That was if she and Bale Mian hadn't quarrelled. But now Bua's eyes had an empty look, like dried-out, smoking oil wicks. A staleness hung about her. Some time had passed since her treatment, but Hakim Sahib's tablets seemed to have become permanently glued to her stomach lining; she would get the runs frequently and was always burping.

There was a time when Bua had the appetite of a bird, but now she heaped her plate high with maize bhat and arhar dal and constantly complained of heartburn. She also spent the better part of the day asleep; leaning against a wall, her mouth open, she could be found sleeping quietly most of the time. In her state of madness she didn't seem to need sleep, now she dozed all day. She had also become quite shrewd. Every day she visited her tenants and bickered with them.

"The bastards aren't paying rent on time, they're out to rob me."

As soon as Bua regained her sanity, she saw that the world was full of thieves and brigands. Her vision cleared and brightened, as if someone had applied a magical kohl to her eyes. The roof was leaking, but who can you get to repair it? All the workers are thieves, they'll clean you out.

After the bracelets came a matching gold necklet with the same lion's head, and this too was immediately placed in Amma's steel safe. Still she wasn't satisfied; every once in a while she'd ask about her jewellery.

"You're sure the lock's working?"

If a robbery took place in the neighbourhood, Bua felt the world was coming to an end. Right away she would have Amma open the safe and check its contents. No longer was she our dear, sweet Bua; she seemed to us now like all other stupid women.

All old associations slowly slipped from our minds. We were irritated by the sight of Bua grinding spices. Clamouring to sleep with her now seemed like a foolish thing to do. Instead of the fragrant odour of freshly-dug earth, her body now gave off an offensive smell of garlic, onions and stale food.

Meanwhile, Aunt Qudsia blossomed some more.

Nani Biwi tried every trick in the book, but Aunt Qudsia did not take the laxative and openly solicited Uncle Shabir's help in reading Mir's poetry. Evening came. No sooner had Aunt Qudsia turned her face to the left with the salaam at the end of the *asr* prayers than Uncle Shabir appeared magically at the front door like the storybook giant. He would explain and she would understand; their eyes remained lowered, their faces wearing masks of strangeness. Their eyes met just once or twice and, for no apparent reason, our hearts raced like colourful kites entwining cords in the sky.

If we, the children, could guess what was going on, surely Nani Biwi, who was exceedingly clever, was not fooled. Dadi Amma, meanwhile, didn't spare her meaningfully judgemental smiles.

'I say, woman, if something untoward happens, the head of the household will have to face dishonour."

Dadi Amma proceeded to explain the intricacies of philosophy to smelly old Pathani Bua while the woman pressed her feet. She raised the subject as if they were discussing everyday politics. God help her, she wasn't pointing to anything specific, but it wouldn't be her fault if suspicion was raised by what she was saying.

Nani Biwi heard all this and fumed.

"Please, break off some tamarind pods, won't you? We'll make some chutney." Aunt Qudsia was playing with the buttons on her shirt front.

Uncle Shabir had just arrived.

"What shall I break them off with? Is there a stick or a pole around here?"

"My word! You're no less than a pole yourself, why don't you just reach up and break some?"

For a split second a rod of brightness flashed in Uncle Shabir's eyes. He appeared alive, and if no one had been around he would certainly have done what Manjhuji's fiance did when he found himself alone with her...

After Uncle Shabir left, Nani Biwi reprimanded Aunt Qudsia for her flighty behaviour.

"Why, have I committed adultery?" snarled Aunt Qudsia.

"Tsk, tsk, you wretch! What will people say? Agreed that Shabir is a decent man, he's not an outsider, he's your brother-in-law, but the world is an unjust place. It doesn't take long for a mole-hill to become a mountain."

"What do I care about the world? For ten years that man—may he die—has been making me weep and no one says one word of reproach to him."

It's true, girls should not read such peculiar books. There's all kinds of rubbish in them.

"Child, he's a man, no one can harm him. A woman's person is like a mirror, once there's a crack in it you'll forever see a crooked image of yourself."

"Hunh!" Unable to pursue the argument further, Aunt Qudsia turned her attention to the box of bangles. *"My Girdhar Gopal/ There is no other..."* she began humming as she selected bangles to match the colour of her shirt.

"The vine has spread, what can anyone do now...My Girdhar..."

"My word, child! How many times have I told you not to sing these dreadful, profane songs? And you neglected the afternoon prayers, too. I tried to wake you up, but you were too lazy. Of course, when you stay up so late at night you're sure to sleep late in the morning, like a bat."

Aunt Qudsia rose to her feet so abruptly her dupatta fell to the floor and the tiny bells on her buttons jingled. Picking up the lota she went to wash for prayers. Nani Biwi was not the only one who was upset; all good women were disturbed by the sight of girls striding about brazenly. Decent girls walked respectfully, taking small steps. Aunt Qudsia's newfound agility had shaken Nani Biwi to the core.

"I say girl, what kind of a gait is this, like a singing girl's, the front and back all sticking out?"

~

Trying to talk to Aunt Qudsia was like hitting oneself with a shoe. Nani Biwi conspired with Amma.

"This wretch Shabir just won't leave us alone. I've told him off so many times, but I think he's not budging because of encouragement from Qudsia. I'm very worried."

"I say, Amma, you're just imagining things. Now you're suspicious of poor Shabir. Because of him the unhappy girl gets to laugh and relax a little. She must have a reason to continue living, don't you think?"

If Amma was in a good mood Nani Biwi became more agitated.

"To hell with such living! What is she planning anyway? And seeing your sister's false tears, you're melting too?"

"I ask you, why would such a thing be so terrible?" Amma said after a pause.

"What do you mean?"

"Machu was saying, he had consulted with a lawyer friend of his, he was saying…"

Uncle Machu's real name was Mustaqeem and his nickname was Machu. Mustaqeem means straight; but Uncle Machu didn't have a straight bone in his body. He was crooked beyond measure.

"May the contemptible wretch's mouth burn! What is he but a good-for-nothing raised on the crumbs of prostitutes!" Nani Biwi went so far as to dig up his grave. He, in the meantime, alive and well, was receiving a hair massage from Aunt Qudsia.

"All right, please…" Amma fumbled for words.

"How dare you! Do you want your sister to have a second husband?"

"Get out of here!" Finding me listening intently to this conversation, Amma smacked me.

Unaware of what was going on, Aunt Qudsia, at that moment, was blushing in response to something Uncle Machu had asked. Just when her glowing, white cheeks seemed to disappear into the folds of her pink dupatta, the curtain moved and Uncle Shabir erupted into the room.

The air around us seemed to hold its breath. Gathering the front folds of her wide-legged pajama, Amma tucked them in at the waist and, ready to serve her lord and master, left the room. The bell on Abba's cycle could be heard from a distance. On his return from the club he usually went straight upstairs to his room, calmly keeping to himself on the second storey, very much like the leader of a caravan. Her keys jangling, Amma strode off to wait upon her husband and Nani Biwi took charge of the fort.

Uncle Machu generally slipped away as soon as he heard the sound of the bell. He was terrified of his serious, sober older brother and made every effort to stay out of his way in order to avoid being questioned on one matter or another. Considering the sort of thing he was involved in, it was certainly prudent for everyone to refrain from questioning him.

Placing the bundle of books on the bed, Uncle Shabir mumbled something, Aunt Qudsia inaudibly mumbled a reply, and off he went to pay his respects to Dadi Amma.

Nani Biwi was on guard for him like a cat waiting to pounce on a mouse. As soon as he emerged from the veranda, she grabbed him.

Aunt Qudsia, feeling a little bashful, walked off to the kitchen to prepare a tray for Abba. Food was being dished out and, presuming that Nani Biwi was sharing some pleasant secrets with Uncle Shabir, she started humming.

The drum had been refurbished. Aunt Qudsia sat down on the

divan, picked it up and proceeded to tighten its rings. Leaning wearily against a wall, periodically spitting on the floor to one side, was Bua; perhaps she wanted to spit out the taste of amaltas from her mouth. These days she would start spitting wherever she was sitting.

"Bua dear, please play the beat you heard at the theatre, show me how the man struck the drum with his palm."

Bua cast a glance at the drum as if asking, "What is this thing?" and then, turning, spat on the floor.

"Oh, Bua! For Bale Mian's sake," Aunt Qudsia implored, pushing the drum towards her. She reached for Bua's hand, pulled her, then hastily let go. "Bua! You have fever!"

When she touched Bua's forehead she discovered it was burning.

Nani Biwi had been complaining for many days that Bua had stunk up her veranda. "I can't breathe," she said, "tell her to go back to her own house, the tenants have gone, we'll send her two meals a day."

She egged on Amma who had lost interest in Bua by this time. Whatever they had all done for her had been done for her own good. Abba had been warning us about tightening our belts. This constant waiting upon guests was taking its toll; we had guests every day, elaborate dishes were prepared, clothes were made for them depending on whether it was summer or winter, and in the end the guests, barely escaping indigestion, grabbed their gifts and left, vacating their beds for a new set of visitors.

Bua's future had been satisfactorily taken care of. It was no one's fault that she wasn't well. Why, didn't she eat everything and anything that came her way? Her sweepress had been gone a long time. The woman did visit once, pressed Bua's feet, crying all the while at her condition, but she was scolded and driven away again. She made her home under a peepal tree and eked out a living by begging.

But now they had no choice.

Manjhu was coming to attend Urs along with her-in-laws. Her mother-in-law wanted to pray and make an offering at the shrine for a grandchild. So Bua returned to her house. However, her precious sweepress became a constant presence on the veranda again. Three times a day, tea and food were set in a tray and sent out. If Bua was feeling well, she'd come herself and stay for several days in a row. Since Nani Biwi had had her veranda whitewashed, she had become extremely cautious; Bua hesitated to be about in such a clean and tidy place. There was a time when Bua's clothes were whiter and cleaner than those donned by the lady of the house and when she visited she sat with the other women. Now when she appeared, a small wooden stool or a bamboo chair was quickly pushed towards her. She either sat on the stool or if one wasn't around, she'd seat herself in the doorway, just like the sweepress, washerwoman, or any other low-caste person.

Sometimes, when she didn't have the energy to make it back to her house, Bua slept in the cowshed, a part of her cot inside the shed, the rest sticking out. The foul smell from Bua's body was lost in the stench of cow-dung and chicken droppings.

~

Uncle Shabir disappeared after his talk with Nani Biwi. Aunt Qudsia paced about restlessly and it seemed that she had vowed not to sleep; all night long she tossed and turned. Nani Biwi was beside herself with anxiety.

About this time Sanjhli's fate once again showed signs of changing. Her prospective in-laws had come and were being appropriately entertained.

"I say, is she the one whose husband brought in a mem?" the prospective sister-in-law inquired in a sorrowful tone.

Instead of trembling with pride, for the first time in her life Aunt Qudsia laughed crudely at this remark. "Yes, sister, my rival is a mem, but I hear yours is an oil-manufacturer's daughter."

This was true, but it was something that had been covered up like cat's shit. The sister-in-law burst into tears.

When the guests left it was discovered that the young man in question had a squint in one eye. But everyone was sure it was Aunt Qudsia who had created a hurdle for Sanjhli this time. When Hakim

Sahib was consulted on the matter of Aunt Qudsia's condition, he presented the same diagnosis as before: an excess of melancholic matter in the body. As for treatment, it was that same wretched amaltas prescription, the only cure for heat in the blood!

Nani Biwi ignored Aunt Qudsia's protests and, setting up a brick stove in her veranda, she prepared the elixir with her own hands.

"Child, say 'Allah is all, Allah will help' and toss it down." Nani Biwi handed her the copper bowl and patted her back.

Aunt Qudsia calmly flung the bowl exactly where Bua had thrown it that day, in the gutter.

"A curse upon you! What are you doing!" Nani Biwi screamed, but Auntie walked away, calmly took the drum off the hook and began humming a song she had learned recently from the sweepress.

Furious, Nani Biwi tried to snatch the drum from Auntie, who pushed her away with such force she nearly lost her balance and fell.

"If I'm a burden for you why don't you bury me alive, why do you want me to die like a dog? I will not drink this poison, I will never drink it!"

That was the day Aunt Qudsia discovered how Nani Biwi had instructed Uncle Shabir, in very polite tones, to stop coming to the house.

"You consider her your sister, dear boy, but people are very narrow-minded…" she explained to him and Uncle Shabir understood.

"Are you out of your mind, wretch!"

"Why shouldn't I be out of my mind? I'm human, I'm not a stone. You hurled me into hell when I was fifteen, the colour of my wedding henna hadn't yet faded when he crossed the seven seas to a faraway place, and there he was stung by a white snake. But tell me, is this all my fault? Did I dally with anyone, did I give a thought to another man?"

"You were destined for a tragic fate! Who can interfere with God's will?"

"What sin have I committed that I should be punished while that scoundrel continues to lead a happy life?"

"You miserable creature, aren't you ashamed to call your husband a scoundrel…he's your earthly God."

"A curse upon his face, the worst villain that ever lived!" Aunt Qudsia advanced threateningly.

"You wretched girl! Have you no pride in your wedded state? He hasn't done anything wrong, the Shariah allows a man to have four wives. You are not the only one in this world, there are thousands who suffer like you, but they endure hardship gracefully. A man is unfaithful by nature."

Finding that she was losing ground, Aunt Qudsia began to curse herself.

"O Allah! Please take me from this world! Mighty ruler, make my body dirt so I can at least be rid of this hell, or else take his life so I can be rid of the vile creature."

"You witch! Who is this you're cursing?" Nani Biwi shuddered. A husband is, after all, a husband.

"Baqar Hussain, your beloved son-in-law, the bastard, the son-of-a-bitch!" Aunt Qudsia was sliping away. "May he burn in hell! May worms gnaw at him in the grave!" Spreading out her dupatta, she swayed as she cursed.

"So, will you go after a second husband?"

"Yes, I will… I will…" No, this wasn't Aunt Qudsia, this was an ogress.

"Then go and sell yourself in the bazaar!"

"I will do that, I dare anyone to stop me."

Aunt Qudsia had no intention of selling herself, but anger led them from one thing to another. Nani Biwi remembered Nana Mian and cried bitterly. Ever since Uncle Shabir had stopped coming to the house, mother and daughter engaged in altercations of this nature nearly every day. Finally Aunt Qudsia's in-laws received news of what was going on. Her father-in-law expressed alarm.

"Amma has spoiled her thoroughly. If this continues any longer the girl will no doubt bring dishonour to the family. It's better that we send for her, she'll come to her senses when she's here."

Nani Biwi agreed to send her. She could no longer bend her to her will. "Yes, this is how it should be," she decided, "it's between them and their daughter-in-law. How much longer can I wrack my brains, anyway?"

But as soon as she heard that her in-laws had sent for her, Aunt Qudsia became enraged.

"Why doesn't he rebuke his son, the hypocrite! May his beard go up in flames, may his face burn!"

"You wretch, he's your uncle!" Nani Biwi screamed.

"To hell with such an uncle! Couldn't say one word of reproach to his own son. I say, they're very happy, there's a mem in the house, they butter her up, sit down at a table to eat dinner with forks and knives. After all, they're living on the crumbs their son throws them, they have to wag their tails in the mem's presence. She's going to make God bless them in the next life no doubt, they're sure to follow even her shadow into heaven."

"You won't stop this nonsense, wretch? O God, save this miserable creature from dishonour. May your tongue burn!" Nani Biwi picked up a shoe and crushed Aunt Qudsia's lips with it.

That was when Aunt Qudsia became like a woman possessed by a ghoul from the cremation grounds. She gnashed her teeth and, grasping both of Nani Biwi's twiggy wrists, she twisted them.

For a split second Nani Biwi peered into her raging eyes. Her heart convulsed. She could not see her dearer-than-life Qudsia Bano there; instead she saw a wounded lioness, a female cobra whose hood had been crushed, and she felt her own life was being squeezed by that steely grasp. The old woman doubled over in fear. Everyone ran towards them with cries of "Hai! hai!" Nani Biwi was trembling from head to foot like a doe surrounded by hunting dogs.

"O God, Qudsia, what have you done? You raised your hand to Amma!"

Feeling completely helpless, Aunt Qudsia struck her hands against the stone slab laying on the terrace, smashing her bangles to pieces.

"I say, people, what is going on?" Dadi Amma, who was deaf, asked impatiently in a stifled voice. "Girls, will someone turn up the wick on the lamp. What is happening?" She was surrounded by lanterns, but who could dispel the darkness in her eyes?

The whole house was in an uproar; all the servants crowded near the front door, the women lifted their pajama folds and ran, the children began to whimper, the hens cackled.

"If anyone comes near me, I swear upon the Quran, I'll split her head open!" Aunt Qudsia lifted the stone slab above her head. All the women valued their lives; they continued to rant and rave, but no one dared take one step in her direction. Aunt Qudsia started crushing the broken pieces of glass. Before she could bring her hand to her mouth, Uncle Shabir calmly placed his hand on her shoulder.

For ten years no man had touched her. Her hands fell limply to her sides. She turned and looked into Shabir Hassan's eyes. This was the moment when she would have even returned from heaven. Closing her eyes, she swooned and fell upon his chest.

Shabir Hassan's worthless hands hesitated for a split second. Then, in front of everyone, he clasped her to his breast with a force that made his ribs crack. The whole family was silenced as if a snake had been spotted. We forgot our play and gaped with our mouths hanging open. The air around us was stilled. Nani Biwi collapsed like a weak roof.

"What is going on, why this sudden silence?" Dadi Amma felt under her pillow for the *sajdah-gah*. "Is everyone getting ready for prayer, is that why no one says a word?"

Shabir Hasan gathered Qudsia Bano's slender body in both arms. It seemed as though he would never let her go, that he would carry her off somewhere. We were all holding our breath. Steeling himself, he gently put her down on the bed and, calmly stationing himself some distance from her, proceeded to stare at the floor as if to say, 'Well, here lies Qudsia Bano, she's unconscious, this is a good opportunity, come quietly and quickly strangle her, but don't kill her slowly, agonisingly.'

~

Hakim Sahib checked her pulse and immediately came to the conclusion that the heat had travelled to her head, causing her brain to become numb. No one has any say in what Allah has fated, he added.

"The hakim speaks nonsense," smelly Pathani Bua remarked as she dusted her lehnga, "it looks like something else to me."

"Yes, I suspect that the sprit that had bewitched that wretch, Bua, has abandoned her and taken over the poor girl instead. Don't you see, sister, as Bua's condition improved poor Qudsia Bano's ways deteriorated." Aunt Baqar did her best to convince Nani Biwi. "What a terrible thing it was to see—the girl would wear white clothes, attar and aromatic oils and wander in the garden at all times of the day."

Aunt Qudsia's status began to improve. She was no longer alone. A sprit, demon, jinn, or some saint was with her. My poor Amma was taken in right away. Amma was a simple soul, anything she didn't understand she feared as a matter of caution.

Saint, demon, sprit or jinn, whatever it might be, she was reluctant to lock horns with any one of them. This was why she regularly sent a donation to the temple for Vishnu and, every now and then, made arrangements to provide fodder for a five-legged cow and milk for snakes.

"Daughter, this is blasphemous," Nani Biwi used to warn her, "offerings and niaz is one thing, but don't ruin your chances of going to heaven by getting involved with these good-for-nothing rituals."

But Amma was more concerned about her husband's life and the well-being of her children than she was about life after death. Now, who was to say that you could do anything if the gods and goddesses got upset? Right next to the cemetery were the cremation grounds and the children wandered around all day like bulls let loose. One day they went into a temple and showed disrespect to Bhagvan. Mahantji came to the door with complaints, and to make amends Amma immediately made arrangements to feed a few Brahmins so that the god would not turn things upside down in anger. Whenever prasad arrived from the temple, all the women in the house said, "Thu, thu, throw it to the hens, it's impure." But Amma would set it down on one of the shelves and in a twinkling the children gobbled it up. Only then was she satisfied. Anyway, children can digest even stones and, who knows, maybe there was something propitious in the prasad.

And now she set out to serve Aunt Qudsia. Agreeing to everything anyone said, she organised incantations and invocations to get rid of jinns, spirits and demons. She also offered niaz in the name of holy saints and began treating Aunt Qudsia with undue regard. She was afraid of this new Qudsia. On the question of madness she was neutral; who knows, maybe the insane also held special powers. Someone with children and a family had to exercise extreme caution in order to avert the threat of danger from any source. And jinns were known to be temperamental; after all, God almighty made man from clay and the jinns from fire; if the fire was ignited who can say what the consequences might be.

It was quite obvious that the spirit or demon that possessed Aunt Qudsia was not the type that would instruct her to throw the shit around. No, she seemed to be under the influence of some very cultured, fashionable, extremely fanciful saint. Uncle Machu writhed when he saw the way Aunt Qudsia was pampered; true, God had not shaped him from fiery flames, but he must surely have used embers.

"I say, Qudsia Bano, what a clever one you are! You're fooling everybody, aren't you?" Uncle Machu smiled, but it was common knowledge that he was a worthless person and an apostate. Everybody cursed and rebuked him.

"The saint will convulse and collapse as soon as you administer three of Hakim Sahib's racking purgatives." He made poisonous remarks, causing Nani Biwi to beat her forehead in distress.

"May your tongue burn! That unfortunate girl has lost her senses and all you can think of is this gibberish." She felt very maternal towards her daughter these days. At the slightest provocation a lump would form in her throat and she would start reminiscing about Nana Mian. "If he were alive would the poor girl have had to listen to such nonsense from people?" she complained one day while preparing a fruit drink for Aunt Qudsia.

"Ah, I understand her wiles. Shabir Mian is the reason for…"

Aunt Qudsia, in the middle of combing her hair, turned to spar with him. She looked into his eyes and sneered.

"Why, did Mushtri Jan beat you with a shoe and throw you out of her house?" she mocked. Everyone was aware that Uncle Machu lived off the earnings of the nautch girls.

"Let's not talk about me, let's talk about you instead…"

"Qudsia, my child," Nani Biwi handed her the glass of sharbat and, turning her face away from Uncle Machu, said, "Don't bother with this wretch, he's a worm from the gutter and he thinks everyone else is like him." After the accident Nani Biwi had become extremely pro-Qudsia.

"The young lady is under the spell of a very powerful saint, he should, under no circumstances, be antagonised," Nani Biwi's Maulana from Lucknow stated emphatically. And Hakim Sahib ventured that in his humble opinion the purgatives should be postponed for the time being; it was important, he maintained, that emotions not be inflamed, otherwise more heat would travel to the brain. But how could you explain all this to Uncle Machu? Ever since she had become unstable, Aunt Qudsia had been enjoying a life of ease and comfort. It was as if she were living on a soft, cottony cloud. Like a princess she reclined all day on a bed that was draped with clean, sparkling sheets, and enjoyed the poetry of Zauq and Sauda; Uncle Shabir sat nearby and recited verses in sweet, mellifluous tones. Once in a while, just to make him uncomfortable, she asked him to explain a suggestive verse. He came regularly now as he had done in the past, and if he was even a few minutes late Aunt Qudsia became restless.

Uncle Machu frequently stooped to low tricks, but that day he went too far. Aunt Qudsia was holding the glass of sharbat to her mouth but hadn't taken a sip as yet.

"What a silly one he is, your Shabir Hasan. Now if it had been me…" He spoke softly in order to avoid being overheard by Nani Biwi.

"If it had been you…?" Aunt Qudsia ground her teeth.

"I'd run off with you," Uncle Machu said, stretching his long arms.

"You miserable wretch! Do you think I'm like Mushtri Jan?" Aunt Qudsia was like an unsheathed sword.

"There's a Mushtri Jan hidden in every woman, and when the opportunity arises…"

Aunt Qudsia flung the glass of sharbat at his face and then, taking off her slipper, she attacked him.

If one can obtain the kingdom of heaven and earth by losing one's mind, who would be stupid enough to want to regain sanity? In the past if Aunt Qudsia happened to raise her voice she was immediately taken to task. Today she was hitting a six-foot tall man built like a giant, cursing him a hundred times in one breath, and everyone was silently applauding.

"Wait, wait, good woman, I was only joking," Uncle Machu said, trying to ward off her blows with his hands. This was the Uncle Machu who had once, for the sake of Mushtri Jan, lifted Sadeeq, the wrestler, and thrown him over a wall as if he were a bunch of flowers, not a man as big as an elephant. This same Uncle Machu was being beaten by Aunt Qudsia. We too were convinced that day that it wasn't delicate little Aunt Qudsia who was pounding Uncle Machu with the force of a wrestler, but indeed the jinn who was in love with her. And who could take on someone who is the beloved of a jinn?

In the twinkling of an eye the different domains of the house became disconnected like unrelated districts. The time for Urs was approaching. In addition to other festivals and celebrations, this too, was an excuse for visitors to appear. Relatives and distant acquaintances began showing up months in advance. But it didn't make much difference since no one was given separate bedrooms or bathrooms. Additional cots, beds and wooden divans were set out and that was all. The tablecloth was lengthened and two people were served in one plate. None of this was a nuisance, except that the atmosphere that prevailed was like that of a noisy, crowded bazaar. Which was a lot of fun. Our maternal camp and that from our father's side of the family were split into smaller groups. It was a strange spectacle. The women who congregated in Dadi Amma's camp were mostly elderly ladies who became agitated if you made the slightest movement in their presence. In Amma's camp were women of her own age, giddy and worldly. Those with husbands and nursing infants were cloistered in a far corner on two beds each, while young girls slept on the opposite side of the veranda, two to a bed. When they were not sleeping, these girls traipsed around like a herd, whispering in each other's ears. Children, hens, pigeons and dogs gathered in the centre of the courtyard and noisily jumped up and down on empty rope cots. If an accident occurred in one part of the house, it would be quite a while before everyone got wind of it.

This was why there were very few eye-witnesses to the beating Uncle Machu received at Aunt Qudsia's hands that day. By the time the females donned their shoes and, grabbing the folds of their pajamas, arrived on the scene, there was no trace of the accident that had taken place with the speed of lightning.

When everyone finally gathered, all they could see was Aunt Qudsia snarling, her face covered with her dupatta, and Uncle Machu ducking out of the door, laughing, as if he had just received sugary sweetmeats, not a sound beating.

"Is anyone listening? What is going on, girls, no one tells me anything." Dadi Amma groaned. All the tired, elderly women in her veranda turned over once on their sides and then continued dozing.

"What is it, what happened?" everyone was asking.

No one knew if smelly Pathani Bua had had an altercation with the cleaning boy upstairs, or if a snake had been spotted somewhere in the house.

"Who was beating whom?" they turned and asked each other again. Mothers were counting their children while Amma, oblivious of all this confusion, her pajama tucked in, had heard the bell on Abba's carriage and was off to meet her beloved.

"What could have happened? Lot of fuss about nothing, that's all!" Although she was one of the few eye-witnesses, Nani Biwi disclosed nothing. "Whoever tussles with these people will suffer," she added mysteriously. She was obviously not referring to Aunt Qudsia. That slip of a girl, so frail and delicate, where could she get the strength! All this was the doing of the saint.

~

It was a very melancholy evening. A thin layer of dust and fog stretched across the sky and swallows scissored the air. The qawwali groups were arriving, all day long workmen repaired large, sprawling marquees, and the shrine, spotlessly white after being whitewashed, looked like an untarnished tent that had been thrown open and spread out unevenly.

During this time we forgot about home and spent the better part of our days at the shrine. The sermon made us cry, but we found the qawwalis extremely enjoyable. We didn't understand a single word of the verses sung, but the mention of Mecca impressed us greatly. Somewhere along the line one of the spectators worked himself into a state of frenzied ecstasy which resulted in widespread commotion. At this time the qawwali singers got stuck at one verse, repeating it over and over again until the person dancing in ecstasy lost his momentum. Then the singers began with a new verse.

"What's the matter, people? Why don't you tell me anything?" As soon as we walked into the house we found Dadi Amma muttering in a confused tone.

Bua's sweepress was touching everyone's feet, begging, "Please come with me, Ram only knows what's happened to her."

"Now calm down, woman, who are you talking about?"

"What happened?" people were asking each other. Finally it was revealed that Bua had been running a fever for several days. The previous night she had left the house and in the morning was discovered lying face down in the cemetery. Since then her windpipe had been rattling.

"Tsk, tsk, the poor thing," the women said sorrowfully and returned to their chores.

"When I ask, no one tells me anything, am I a dog, barking away with no one to hear me?" Dadi Amma retrieved her sajdah-gah from under her pillow and murmured her niyat. Nani Biwi was appalled by the manner in which she recited her intent and also objected to the way Dadi Amma bowed during prayers, claiming she looked like a frog ducking into water.

Aunt Qudsia, the only person who seemed to be in distress, ran anxiously from one corner of the house to another. "Will someone send for the doctor?"

The doctor responsible for cases at the shrine treated patients free of charge. No one was surprised at Aunt Qudsia's perturbation, and no one had the temerity to ignore her command. All night long Bua's windpipe continued to rattle. The doctor diagnosed her condition as double-pneumonia. The next morning we also went to see her, not out of concern for her health but out of curiosity. Stretched out on a worn-out rope cot Bua was struggling for life. The air was so putrid you couldn't breathe. It was only on the third day that the rattling of the windpipe ceased.

May God forgive us! Her body stiff in the white shroud, Bua looked so terrifying! How woebegone and miserable her face was— those half-opened eyes, the purple colouring, that pinkish fluid oozing from her nose and mouth. For years to come she appeared in my dreams to frighten me. I'd be scared to go in the dark, fearful that Bua might suddenly appear and devour me; as soon as it was twilight my spirits flagged and I'd be afraid to go out and pick buds. It seemed as if she was behind the mosque, standing under the banyan tree, dusting off sand from her slipper and I almost expected to see her appear suddenly, singing, "*Beat the drums/Well meet in Meerut...*"

She was always cross with Bale Mian, but when he turned away from her the whole world rejected her. Bua suffered in this terrible manner and not once did he bother to turn around and ask how she was doing. Ah, poor, unfortunate Bua! The world polices dreams as well, the very reason for living becomes a sore point with people.

The terror of Bua's death hung over the entire household. Everyone's hands were stained with Bua's innocent blood. In order to rid the house of evil spirits, two maulvis were immediately stationed in the outer courtyard. All day they rocked while reading from the Quran, and then proceeded to stuff themselves with trayfuls of food.

Bua's death completely unsettled Aunt Qudsia. For two days she ate nothing. All night she paced about restlessly, stared at the floor in the veranda, in the dark, with her head lowered as though in search of a crack that she could disappear into. She gazed about her, wide-eyed like a starving bird, as if afraid that some bloodthirsty animal might spring at her and grab her throat. All around her she saw death. Nani Biwi prepared glasses of sharbat and left them with her and she emptied them into the spittoon when no one was looking. Holding the paan in her hand, she pretended to chew but later threw it into the toilet. She took a morsel or two only from Amma's plate. She no longer trusted anyone.

That evening Uncle Shabir came. For a while he sneaked glances around him like a thief, then, avoiding Aunt Qudsia's gaze, he handed her a copy of *Diwan-e-Ghalib*. After this he greeted Dadi Amma and then left without casting another look at Aunt Qudsia. Tightly clasping the book in both hands, Aunt Qudsia sat still, as though a cobra might leap out of it and devour her if she opened it. Nani Biwi was straightening her bedsheets. She lovingly arranged some flowers on her pillow and turned back the quilt.

"Here, daughter, why don't you rest for a while. I'll bring your food here, there's a lot of rubbish over there." She pointed to the crowd eating at the tablecloths laid out on the veranda floor.

"I'm not hungry, Amma Bi." Aunt Qudsia placed the book under her pillow.

"Why child? You didn't eat anything at lunch either, and…" She had no idea that her daughter was distrustful of her. After all, she was a mother. She had always doted on her favourite daughter, whatever she did was for her own good.

All at once Aunt Qudsia's heart jumped into her mouth. Uncle Machu was picking up the book. She felt as if she was in the grip of a fever. A tiny fragment of paper fluttered and fell at her feet. Before she could retrieve it, Uncle covered it with his shoe, bent down and picked it up, turned it over a few times, then handed it to Nani Biwi. Aunt Qudsia closed her eyes.

"What is it?" Nani Biwi took the fragment from him, glanced at it cursorily and threw it down. "Don't be silly!" Nani Biwi was illiterate, she couldn't read a thing.

"Wait a minute, this is a charm, don't be disrespectful." Uncle Machu took the paper and placed it on Aunt Qudsia's pillow.

"What kind of charm?" Nani Biwi asked in a serious tone.

"It's for getting rid of evil spirits."

"Hunh! I'm not your playmate that you should tease me." Muttering angrily, Nani Biwi left.

"And those who are playmates don't care either," Uncle Machu mumbled softly as he walked off to pay his respects to Dadi Amma.

"Amma Begum, please give me the Fatehpur land or, I swear by Imam Hussain, I'll become a Sunni."

"Some religion!" Nani Biwi grunted under her breath.

"If you give me the Amethi mango gardens right away, I promise I'll become a Sunni," he wrangled with Nani Biwi next.

"Goodness! Those are in Qudsia's name!"

"That's all right, I'll take Qudsia too as a gift, and I'll shut everybody up, don't you worry."

"Dust in your mouth!" Nani Biwi ran after him with her shoe and he shot off to one of our other aunts.

"If you give me these bracelets, I'll cut the noses and plaits of all your rivals and place them at your feet." But no one gave him anything because everyone knew he had wasted his entire inheritance on dancing girls.

Nani Biwi woke up in the middle of the night for *tahajud* prayers and the hands that were raised for ablution remained suspended in mid-air. Aunt Qudsia's bed was empty. The flowers were still on the pillow, untouched, fragrant, not a petal out of place. The front door was ajar like a gaping hole, its latch still swinging. Nani Biwi's screams roused the whole household. She was running around from one corner of the house to the other, yelling Aunt Qudsia's name. Soon everyone picked up lanterns and began the search.

"Will you listen, what's going on, I ask?" Dadi Amma's whimpering query compounded the confusion.

Her arms around her as if she were a little girl, Amma tried to comfort Nani Biwi.

"What's happened?" The question came from all sides. Children began to whine, the hens started cackling.

"Oh, I think someone left the chicken coop open." In her state of drownsiness Dadi Amma came to the conclusion that the cat had made off with one of the hens.

The imprints of Aunt Qudsia's small, bare feet were traced to the edge of the large well, where they disappeared. On the left the path leading to the railway station was full of marks made by animals and people, but there were no signs of Aunt Qudsia's tiny, white feet. The well was searched thoroughly but Aunt Qudsia's body was not found. Had the earth devoured her, the sky swallowed her?

"My daughter was meant for heaven," Nani Biwi wailed, weeping uncontrollably on the third day of mourning.

"Why do you cry? May Allah bless her wherever she is," Uncle Machu said, drying false tears. What a vile man he was, our Uncle Machu!

"Amen." Dadi Amma proceeded to recite verses from the Quran under her breath.

In a few days some rather strange stories began circulating.

When Aunt Qudsia jumped into the well a window suddenly opened in its floor. She saw a vast expanse of open space. Absolute silence reigned around her and there wasn't a soul in sight. All at once a cloud of dust rose in the distance. When the dust settled she saw a golden throne arrayed with richly-embroidered cushions. Four fairies, holding the throne aloft, stood before her respectfully, their heads lowered. Aunt Qudsia was escorted to the throne which then ascended into the sky.

It was Uncle Machu who invented these tales. Some tactless people also suggested that she had run off with Uncle Shabir. Anyway, the mention of Aunt Qudsia's name became taboo in our house from that day on. As long as Nani Biwi was alive no one dared take her name for fear of a rebuke from her. Then everyone forgot everything because forgetting is profitable; your conscience doesn't torment you.

~

About two and a half months ago I received a telephone call.

"My name is Rafiah Hasan. I'm calling from the Victoria Terminus. Tomorrow I'm leaving for London by a morning flight. Do you think you could see me…I won't take too much of your time."

She was going abroad for her Ph.D. I didn't feel like seeing her. She was probably a literary enthusiast and she would reiterate the usual trite views and upset me: well-established writers don't give newcomers a chance, they only praise each other, etc. She would attempt to prove I was biased, that I was an opportunist.

"As a matter of fact…" I tried to hedge.

"I promise I won't stay long, just ten minutes will be sufficient." I could see she was clever.

When she arrived she smiled affectionately at me and for some reason I felt a burden lifting.

"I obtained your address with great difficulty. You probably don't know this, but you're my cousin. My mother, Qudsia Shabir Hasan, is your aunt."

"Aunt Qudsia? You're Aunt Qudsia and Uncle Shabir's daughter?" I stuttered like a fool. *'We'll meet in Meerut/The two of us.'* Bua's melodious voice rattled the doors of memory. So they did meet. Some people die so that others may learn how to live!

"And just then Ammi's courage gave out. She fought with Abba, accused him of trying to lead her astray, but Uncle Mustaqeem…"

"Uncle Machu!" He was not destined for heaven, but God works in mysterious ways.

"Ammi lost her nerve when she saw him. She was on her way to jump into the well and drown herself. But Uncle Machu said, 'You left your shoes behind, you'd better put them on or else you'll catch your death of a cold.'"

"Uncle Machu said that?"

"Yes, and took out Ammi's shoes from his pocket and gave them to her. But Ammi insisted she wanted to die."

"But the imprints of her feet?"

"How could anyone find those? Abba lifted her up in his arms." She burst out laughing. "Whenever I think of this story I can't help laughing. Ammi is so fat now. Well, from there they went to the railway station."

"And from there to Meerut." I was tormented by Bua's memory.

"Meerut? No, to a friend's house in Raduli."

"Raduli? Her in-laws. Well done!"

"Whose in-laws?" She was confused.

"Never mind, continue."

"Abba's friend, Abrar, was a lawyer. They tried very hard to obtain a divorce, but he said, 'I'll die before I divorce her'."

"And how could fate be so cruel—he didn't die."

"It didn't make any difference. He was never really alive anyway."

"You're right, it didn't make any difference."

When all efforts to secure a divorce failed, Uncle Machu's friend came up with the idea that there was a chance of getting a divorce if Aunt Qudsia became a Christian. A priest in Kanpur was consulted. But when he was given the reason for the intended conversion, he was furious. Also, if Aunt Qudsia reverted to Islam later the divorce would be nullified.

Uncle Machu, when he got news of this muddle, arrived on the scene and threw a fit. He threatened to kill everyone and run off with Aunt Qudsia himself. He also threatened to take Uncle Shabir to task. That same evening a maulvi was sent for and the nikah took place.

"'This is not a proper marriage,' Shabir Hasan's friend, Abrar, said. He was a lawyer."

"'Why not?' Uncle Machu was ready to twist Uncle Abrar's neck."

If Aunt Qudsia's husband had got wind of this he could have brought charges of adultery against them.

Aunt Qudsia and Uncle Shabir went into hiding like thieves for the rest of their lives. It's true, ordinary people generally lead anonymous lives but there's always fear, this despite the fact that Uncle Machu had warned Aunt Qudsia's husband that if he gave them the slightest bit of trouble he'd kill him.

"And how will I face God?" Aunt Qudsia used to say.

"You just fall down and faint when you're there, and I'll take care of the rest," Uncle Machu comforted her.

"And when the divorce bill was passed he and his English wife were in England. They had settled there after he obtained British nationality. Also, I wasn't a child anymore. My parents didn't think it was necessary to start a commotion all over again." She became pensive for a few moments. "When I think of Ammi and Abba's love, I feel like laughing at the importance that is attached to marriage and divorce. Perhaps this is because I'm not like everybody else."

"How do you know you're not like everybody else?"

"Because I think what Ammi and Abba did was what they should have done. I consider myself fortunate to be the fruit of their love."

She had come for ten minutes only. But the thought of wishing her goodbye had still not occurred to me and she hadn't mentioned leaving either. A few hours earlier I had had no knowledge of her existence. She was a stranger to me. After dinner we strolled on Marine Drive late into the night, hand-in-hand, like children. A fragrant flower blossomed between us and kept blooming.

"It seems as though we've known each other for years." We were both experiencing the same feeling.

"Sometimes one tiny moment becomes a heavy burden for the rest of life."

"For what crime did Ammi suffer so much?"

A silence hung between us for some moments.

"And why was Bua separated from Bale Mian?"

"Why do people snatch someone else's dreams and crush them?"

"Because there are no dreams in their own barren lives."

"And so they murder others? Why?"

"In order to get rid of their feelings of inferiority they scream and say, 'My country is great, my religion is the most supreme, my city, my house…my world are the best and of the highest order, my consciousness, my beliefs, my way of thinking are right."

"But forcibly?"

"Yes, forcibly. These are the people who regard freedom of action and freedom of thought to be the right of every individual, who advocate democracy, who use swords to stuff democracy down your throat, or call it a divine right, or force it on the pretext of some emotion or principle, some cultural or social standard. And if all fails, they blame spirits and demons."

At the airport the next day we embraced and she clung to me for a long time, as if she wanted to imbue my very being with a special message.

"There's only one thing I hope for."

"What?" The line of passengers was diminishing.

"That we should also have someone to love us with the kind of dedication with which Abba loved Ammi…and…" She lowered her eyes.

"And?" I stopped her at the stairs leading to the boarding gate. If she left without telling me I'd be tormented by the sharp pain of this unfinished sentence for the rest of my life.

"And like Uncle Machu who…"

"Uncle Machu!" Uncle Mustaqeem, that crooked, devious Mustaqeem, the lecher, libertine, apostate, drunkard, liar, who was a running sore on the family's lustrous, elevated forehead, whom no girl in the family would allow to touch even her soiled hem. He had loved Aunt Qudsia, loved her in such a way that today her daughter held in her heart a longing for such a man.

"But he knew Ammi didn't care about anyone except Abba. Poor Abba, he was such a wishy-washy person. The entire scheme had been devised by Uncle Machu."

She left. Suddenly I was engulfed by an immense loneliness.

"Uncle Machu. Did you hear? Right now there must be little fireflies glittering in your grave."

When will people learn to recognise each other's true worth?

The plane shuddered like an irate giant, thundered, and flew off into the lofty sky.

Go, Rafiah Hasan, you can go without fear wherever you want to go. You have your own tape measure, your own weights, your own scales to plot and gauge life's values. No one will be able to cut you down, your dreams will never be crushed.

The Wild One
(*Ziddi*)

Puran

Rain fell with unflagging tenacity. The sky seemed to have developed holes, but was it any wonder really that having been stretched taut for this long it should now come apart? It had rained several nights in a row and today, beginning early in the morning, it had continued to come down all day. It was as if oceans of water were being hurled with great force at the earth. Defenceless now, the mud walls of many of the houses had started collapsing from the impact of the water; roofs swung like soggy beards from the weight of the poles and bamboo rafters, forcing the inmates of these dwellings to seek shelter under trees. But the water appeared to mock them. The trees were not canopies of stone, so why should it not find its escape through branches and leaves? The sound of overflowing drains sharpened the mood of anxiety that prevailed, while darkness, fast approaching, threatened to further exacerbate the situation.

Asha was trying to give Amma a last drink of water. Her own mother had died early, while her father, a good-for-nothing fellow, was found dead some years later near the railway station. Since then Asha's maternal grandmother had been both father and mother to her. But her grandmother was also about to depart. She had been good to her, but now she was old and sick. It was true that at one time she had been Raja Sahib's nurse, and after he passed away she had continued to straddle his children on her shrunken, bony knees and sing the same old worn-out lullabies that she had once amused him with. But she was a servant after all; she hadn't been left with an endowment of land. As for her jewellery, she sold the pieces off one by one when she fell on hard times. She had always lived in Raja Sahib's palace, and anyway, who needs gold trays in one's old age?

Slowly she crumbled away in a corner of the palace until finally, as an act of kindness, Raja Sahib ordered a subsidy for her and sent her back to her village. Whatever else might happen, she was glad that at least she would die in her own place. But it wasn't her village really, it was Raja Sahib's.

"He's not here? He's not here yet?"

Asha thought the old woman was referring to the messenger of death, but in fact she was thinking of Puran. Puran was Raja Sahib's younger son. He had slept in the old woman's bed until he was seven. Every Sunday he came to the village with his older brother and today was Sunday, wasn't it? Why was the old woman waiting for him? If it hadn't been for this, her breath might have abandoned her body a long time ago.

"Where is Ranji's mother?" The old woman came out of her stupor.

"Yes, Amma, shall I get her? It's raining."

"No…but she…shouldn't have left…like this."

Her own breath seemed to be strangling her. "Is it raining hard?" She was worried the rain might hinder the lighting of her funeral pyre.

"Yes." Asha nervously twisted a corner of her dhoti.

"And where is Ranji's mother, the wretch!" Why was she so preoccupied with Ranji's mother?

Ranji's full name was Ranjit; the "Singh" had been added on to veil the stigma associated with the trader caste. But everyone called him just Ranji. His mother had been known at different times as Kirya's bride, Moti's daughter-in-law and Ram Bharosa's wife, and had changed roles quite often. All the men she had been associated with died one by one. Ranji was the offspring of one of these men, and as such his place in society was akin to that of a thor tree; he expressed no desire to be useful. As a teenager he joined a band of singing eunuchs for a period of time. This caused his mother to spend the better part of her day cursing and swearing at the people in her neighbourhood; persistent in her refusal to believe he had anything to do with the eunuchs, she kept telling everyone he was with a nautanki troupe. Whatever it was, after a few weeks Ranji returned to the village and, soon thereafter, gained notoriety for his singing. Also, he suddenly developed a defiant streak; whereas he had once been associated with eunuchs, he now kept company with the worst kind of ruffians. His mother, despite all this, went around the village with her head held high.

The old woman's anxiety bore fruit; Ranji's mother arrived under cover of a gunny sack.

"Where did you go?" the old woman roared like the angel of death.

"It's all right, I went to see if Ranji had returned. I stopped over at Lachmi's mother's place—I don't know where that wretch has taken off to!"

"Hunh! And what if I had died?" The old woman didn't want to frighten Asha by dying when the girl was alone with her. And she was justified in scolding Ranji's mother. After all, Ranji had professed love for Asha. The old woman's first reaction had been indignation. Then she examined her surroundings closely and realised there weren't any wonderful young men forthcoming. Also, although Ranji behaved like a scoundrel in his own home, he had certainly never had the courage to tease Asha. But then Asha rarely left the house. Like a snake the old woman had sat guard over her all these years. Whatever Ranji's mother did for the old woman was in the nature of a bribe. And whenever Ranji came over, he'd sit in a corner like a donkey with his head lowered. The old woman felt inclined to consider him for Asha, but she hadn't quite made up her mind yet. Anyway, Asha was still too young. It was only two years ago that she started wearing a proper dhoti; until then, dressed in a lehnga, she looked like a little girl. But Ranji's mother maintained that the lehnga or dhoti had nothing to do with anything—at Asha's age she had already had two miscarriages and was pregnant for the third time.

"It depends on how one is built," the old woman used to say, impressed by Ranji's mother's pluck. "My Asha is so delicate." And then she would take a look at Ranji's massive physique and shudder fearfully.

Ranji was not a bad man. But who was conducting a beauty

contest? True, he was short and his teeth were slightly inverted; the lower line of teeth protruded while the upper row was pushed in, making his jaw stick out somewhat and when he laughed it seemed as though his throat had been turned upside down. His lips were flat, his nose was broad and bent, and the little hair left on his head was constantly bedraggled from lack of washing. But he had soulful eyes.

"Isn't Puran here yet?" the old woman asked, tired of hearing about Ranji.

"What? Do you think he's going to come in this downpour? Let me tell you, these high-class people don't really care about anyone."

If the old woman had had any spirit left in her she would have come down hard on Ranji's mother, forcing her to swallow her words. The blind wretch! Did she not see him come every Sunday? As soon as he came he would ask for pure butter and pickles. Pure butter in war time? Why did the war make butter disappear? They must be using it to fire their canons...but why don't they use gasohol instead? People have to subsist on gasohol while the canons...yes, these canons, these blazing canons...no sooner do you speak than they start spewing flames, these white men! What is this? What do white men have to do with butter?

Anyway, Puran came every Sunday. Today the old nurse waited anxiously for him and the rain wasn't letting up.

"What do you know? Of course he will come...look, is that him?"

"No, that's not him." Afraid of having to get up and go to the door, Ranji's mother answered quickly. "Now, have you eaten anything?" she asked, making an attempt to change the subject. "Just look how weak you are." She tried to frighten the old woman by reminding her of death.

A few minutes later they heard Raja Sahib's car. The old woman perked up. She recognise the sound of the car well. When did any other car ever come to the village? In a few minutes Puran was sitting beside the old woman in the soiled, foul-smelling bed.

"Amma, you're not getting the proper treatment here," he said lovingly, "I've come to take you home."

The old woman was willing to go with him, but a hand stronger than Puran's was pulling her with increasing force. "I'm going to be with Pramatma soon, son…"

"What kind of talk is this? You're the one who used to say I'll bring home Puran's bride, I'll sing songs to his son, I'll get leave from Pratmatma if I have to… Let's go then, let's go today. You'll get treatment like this!" he said, snapping his fingers.

"No doctor can cure me now…listen, son…"

"No, Amma, you…"

"Listen, my dear child…Asha, my daughter, she's a very good girl, I've taken special care of her…take her to Raja Sahib, don't make her unhappy, find a nice boy for her to marry…people are all the family she has now."

Puran failed to recognise the signs of death. "No, you have to come along."

"I'll go…if only Ranji had been a decent…"

"Ranji is making plans to start his own business with the village lender's help," Ranji's mother spoke up. "It will get going in no time." Although Ranji had made several attempts to run his own shop, the business lasted only as long as the goods in the shop did. When he and his friends consumed whatever was in the shop, Ranji would move on to another enterprise. He set up a dahi-bare stand and finished everything off himself; the paan and cigarette shop was done in by freeloading friends and acquaintances. The initial investment also went down the drain.

"Yes, if Ranji settles down he's not a bad sort at all."

"We'll see, Amma. First you must concentrate on getting well."

But the old woman was not the slightest bit interested in getting well, and even if she was death had no mind to wait any longer. Puran's request became futile when the old woman departed, leaving a sobbing Asha behind.

Ranji's mother let out a fearsome wail which frightened Asha into silence. Who was left to mourn like this? When the tree dried up, the leaves were scattered here and there. Asha got into Puran's car to begin a new life at Raja Sahib's house. All the way there she cowered in a corner, silently wiping her tears. Afraid that her sobbing might increase if he talked to her, Puran left her to herself.

But when Asha arrived at the palace, her wildly thumping heart quietened somewhat. Raja Sahib patted her head lovingly and Mataji made her sit next to her. But Bhabi—Bhabi clasped her to her bosom.

Asha was too young to grieve forever for an old grandmother. In a few days she forgot her pain. The company of the other servants, her own work, and the love she received from Bhabi and the children made her forget everything else as well. Soon she embarked on a simple, peaceful life.

Bhabi

Asha had no brothers or sisters so there was no question of having a bhabi. But whenever she saw the impish, good-natured daughter-in-law of this family, her heart stirred with love. Although petite like a doll, with hands that were small and helpless-looking, Bhabi was mischievous indeed! And how her laughter rang, like silver beads striking against each other. It was difficult to imagine she was mother to these children. Judging from her looks you would think she was only a little older than Nirmal. As a matter of fact, when Nirmal was born she didn't quite know how to wrap a sari. And Sheela! What a cow she was, the stout daughter of a dainty, slender mother. What she ate in one day her mother would not be able to consume in three. And the youngest, he was remarkable! Yes, it wasn't difficult to imagine him as Bhabi's son because he was the one she doted on the most. Such strange children, and then her husband, the image of Buddha! The more she laughed, the quieter he became. A bania's spirit seemed to have invaded his body; he appeared to spend most of his time managing the affairs of the estate. Yes, sometimes he smiled, but that was all. And Bhabi? She soared like a butterfly all day long. Although she and her husband were as different as the sky and earth, they got along well, just as the sky and earth have been getting along since eternity. He wasn't concerned with the fact that his wife was young and stubborn, or that she was temperamental and easily upset by some little thing her mother-in-law might say. She would shut herself up in her room and cry for hours afterwards, or complain to her brother-in-law, and she was such a favourite among her in-laws that her mother-in-law's alleged mistreatment of her was also reported to her father-in-law. As for Puran, she quarrelled with him constantly. He was the first one to win her affection after she was married and came to this house, and he was the one she fought with the most too. She had never learned to be timid.

This Bhabi, spirited and lively, began her day early in the morning with orders that the children bathe and dress. Then she supervised breakfast until she was out of breath.

"Mummy, my toast!" Nirmal screamed. Skinny little boy!

"Where's my milk?" All the milk she drank made Sheela as round as a kachori.

And at this point the baby would emit a scream from some remote corner of his throat. Bhabi wrestled to keep peace between them.

"Look, Mummy, she took my papad," Nirmal bleated.

"Here, take your papad back, you beggar!" Sheela threw the papad at him.

"Mummy, look," Nirmal wailed.

"Dried insect!"

"Fat cow!"

"You dried up insect, the wind's going to blow you away one day."

"You fat cow, one day you're going to burst with a loud bang."

"Dog! Cow!" The two ended up scratching each other's faces. Before long milk spilled on to Sheela's beautiful embroidered frock and a piece of toast got stuck to Nirmal's elbow. This was when Bhabi yelled at them.

"Nirmal, what silliness is this?" Nirmal would receive a couple of smacks on his thigh and Sheela a wallop or two on her back.

And if by any chance Puran happened to wander in, all hell would break loose. He would make Nirmal choke on his food, tickle

Sheela in the stomach and squeeze the baby's chubby cheeks until they were red.

"Get away, who do you think you are," Bhabi would protest, pushing Puran away with her small hands. "My poor baby, his cheeks are so sore from all this pinching."

But Puran proceeded to crush him and the baby continued to giggle.

"Look, Bhabi, he's laughing," Puran would say.

"He has no shame."

"Yes, he's like his mother." Puran would fling the baby in the air, making Bhabi's heart convulse.

"Puran, O Puran, my baby!" She would hold her breath, but when Puran turned the baby's face around she'd see he was still smiling.

And if Asha were given a chore to do Puran would protest: "Asha is not our servant, Bhabi, why do you make her work?"

"Why, don't we do any work?"

"Oh yes, you really work very hard, smacking the children all day long. What else do you do? But Asha is not a servant."

"You don't become a servant simply by working. And anyway, Asha has to get married one day, she's from a poor family, do you think she'll have servants in her home?"

"So what if she's from a poor family. Why does she have to be married to someone poor?"

"If she won't marry someone poor, then you had better find her a prince, Puran Singhji," Bhabi spoke in a loud voice so everyone could hear her. Puran lost his nerve.

"That's not what I mean, you're raising your voice for no reason. Why do you have such an enormous throat?" Puran muttered and took his revenge by turning again to Munna's cheeks and Sheela's stomach.

Chote Bhaiya

There was an old saying that if you eat fiery hot peppers while you're pregnant, your baby will have a peppery temperament when he grows up. Perhaps when Bari Bahuji was carrying Puran she had chewed on some hot peppers. He could not be still for a moment. There was no problem when he was away at college, but when he came home during the holidays, he brought a storm in his wake. Having finished college, he was permanently home now, preparing for the civil service exam. Who knows why he had taken this silly notion into his head. The family's land holdings and assets were enough for seven generations of comfortable living. But once boys go to college their attitude towards life in the village changes. Actually, the fault lies with the villages themselves. What can they offer besides land cultivation and management to hold misshapen, dilapidated cottages, muddied paths, putrid streams, revolting rows of cow-dung cakes, sickly-looking livestock, and soiled children. How can one be happy there?

Anyway, Puran didn't have a quiet bone in his body. All day long he locked horns with Bhabi, teased the children, clowned around with the female help, and sneaked in sarcastic comments about Bare Bhaiya.

"Bhabi, I've heard that a black cat crossed our mother's path when Bhaiya was about to arrive in this world."

"Hunh! Do you think he should be a good-for-nothing like you? And stop tickling my daughter, her stomach's not made of stone."

"All you ever think about are the children. Do you give any thought to their father? It's true that the children can't be ignored, but what about your dear husband? He putters around with the accounts ledger all morning. I'm sure he laughs sometimes, perhaps when he's by himself…"

"I am going to hit you, Puran, you wretch!" The idea of Bhaiya laughing in private proved to be so funny that Bhabi blushed.

Bare Bhaiya was not the only one who bore the brunt of his teasing. Puran went after the servants as well, especially Chamki, who often received a playful smack from him. Sometimes he splattered her face with shaving cream while he shaved, or tied her braid to the bedpost. All right, she was a young woman so she enjoyed his teasing, but what did he have in common with Bhola's aunt? Frail of mind, she lay in a corner of the veranda all day long like a pile of abandoned debris. In winter she covered herself with an old coat or sweater, but in the sizzling summer heat even her kurta became too much for her. Since she couldn't tolerate the humidity in her room she chose to doze on the veranda instead, fanning herself with a broken fan. Puran often went and sat beside her.

"Do you hear me, Bhola's aunt? Why throw your youth in the dust?"

The old woman glared at him in the hope that he would take her indifference as a hint and leave her alone.

"Do you hear me, you're still so young."

"Go away, boy."

"Now this is what I don't like, listen to me..."

"What do you want?" Bhola's aunt's voice was like that of an old man's.

"What I'm saying is, why don't you wear a kurta?" Puran said, unable to come up with any other criticism.

The old woman stubbornly ignored his remark. The young servant girl blushed at this, and Bhabi also pretended she hadn't heard anything.

"I'll get you something, if you like I can get you three or four blouses."

"Be off, you and your blouses!" There was no change in the old woman's bad humour.

"How many times have I said, Bhola's aunt, you should apply some mehndi and kajal." The young girls giggled and Bhola's aunt muttered coarse invectives under her breath.

"These witches are jealous of you, Bhola's aunt." And slowly Puran inched closer to the old woman.

"What is this? Get away, son."

"You're calling me 'son'?" Puran pretended to be seriously offended.

"Yes, brother, now be a good boy and sit over there, it's too hot."

"Now you're calling me 'brother'?" Puran feigned further indignation.

"Shouldn't call you son, shouldn't call you brother, so should I call you husband?"

And once again the old woman let loose a tirade of invectives.

"I suggest we get married. Now, how old are you?"

"Wretch! Don't court trouble, bastard!" The old woman roared in a heavy voice.

"Bhola's aunt, when you start swearing, I want to kiss you. Wonderful! Excellent!"

Finding that her swearing was ineffective, Bhola's aunt resorted to physical retaliation. All the young servant girls became involved in the scuffle, the old woman continuing to spew a torrent of such foul language that even Puran finally made off from there in embarrassment. When she took her complaints to Bari Bahuji, Bhabi teased:

"Well, why don't you, Bhola's aunt? He's not such a bad boy."

And Bhola's aunt retorted with something that made Bhabi bolt from the room.

Chamki

Chamki came from the same village as Asha. Her name was Chamki because every other girl in the village was called Chamki. If you saw a girl who had a squint, was small and dark, you would think her name might be Kallu or Radhu or something similar. But no, she would turn out to be Chamki. Chamki, however, was indeed Chamki; her cheeks shone, her eyes shone, and as for her hair, it shone like strands of polished steel. As a matter of fact, her waist shone too, as did her hands, and when she danced it seemed as though she was surrounded by dancing stars. Her voice was loud and melodious, not meek and cowering like Asha's which could put you to sleep. Her voice roused people from their dreams, and if she went out, all the orderlies, stewards and gatekeepers began humming; not only that, the dhobi's arms rippled with renewed energy and the sound of his humming grew louder. But she wore an angry look when she was out of the house and ignored everybody, so that if the Munshi, who at least had an F.A., ogled her, she abruptly turned away from him as well. Of course, when her back ached from Puran's pummelling, she seemed to bloom. And what a disorderly person he was! None of the menservants could keep his room in order. He turned the whole cupboard upside down when he took something out, and while looking for one pair of shoes, would toss out five or six others, scattering them all over the room. His books would be strewn about like a scattered deck of cards and his dressing table, always dripping wet and splattered all over with shaving lather. If Chamki cleaned his room he rewarded her by spanking her or tweaking her cheeks.

Like a diligent supervisor, she began making preparations to clean his room early in the morning. If there wasn't anything else to be done, and while Asha was busy helping out with rolling puris, Chamki would spend her time arranging fresh flowers in Puran's room so that it resembled a garden.

First these young women throw themselves before an oncoming train, then you have moaning and groaning followed by complaints that they have been disgraced, dishonoured and robbed. Thus they hold society responsible for their own weaknesses, and how strange that the world chooses to participate in their mourning and proceeds to join in their condemnation of society. So Chamki, too, threw herself before the train. Luckily this engine changed tracks and went its way. Puran's game didn't go beyond pummelling and occasional pinching. But thunder will bring down rain some day. Anyway, the other female servants in the house didn't approve one bit of Chamki's tomfoolery with Puran. Cutting remarks and comments were exchanged all day long:

"Well, haven't you seen a cat playing with a mouse, and the stupid mouse thinks it's just play?" Lata was very philosophical and why not, she was the mother of six children.

"Wait and see, she's always in there with him, she'll not forget, these princes are no good…" Bhola's aunt was not Chamki's rival.

Asha paid little heed to what was being said, but there was no doubt that she was afraid of Puran. She remembered that one day he had sauntered in while she was mending Sheela's frock and started a conversation with her.

"Work, work! I say, Asha, why don't you ever do something for me too?"

"What do you want me to do?" Asha bent over the machine.

"There are thousand of things to be done. For example, the dhobi brings back my wash with nearly all the buttons missing and I have to go around with my shirt-front open."

"What buttons?" Chamki interjected sharply. "I stitched on every last one."

"I'm not talking to you! You see, Asha, you've never done a thing for me. Anyway, why should you be working at all? Are you a servant?"

"Everyone has to work—you don't work, you don't eat." Chamki vied for Puran's attention, but he was only interested in Asha.

"You're so frail and thin and you have to do all the work. I'm going to speak to Mataji, I'll tell her she shouldn't make you work so hard, and…"

"No, please…I like working."

"And why don't the others do some work, too? This Chamki, for instance, such a cow, why isn't she sewing?"

Chamki was sitting nearby hemming Bhabi's sari. Asha cowered under the weight of Puran's burning gaze.

"That's enough now," Puran said, snatching the frock from her hands.

"No…" Asha wished she could disappear into the machine.

"I forbid you to continue sewing!"

"Sheela is going out, she's in a hurry."

"There's no hurry."

Asha remained silent.

"All right, there, go ahead and sew right over this." Puran placed his finger next to the needle on the machine.

"A curse upon these scissors!" Chamki flung her scissors down and left the room in a huff.

"What is that witch so worked up about? Here, Asha, let me see, did she hurt your hand? I'll see to that miserable creature in a minute."

"Chote Bhaiya, we'll never be done with the housework if you keep meddling like this." Chamki's defeat had amused Lata.

"What a grouse you are, Lata. Am I talking to you or…"

"I wish you had been outside, instead of sitting here wasting your time with these girls." It was Bare Bhaiya, standing in the doorway.

Embarrassed, Puran quickly busied himself with extinguishing his cigarette.

"For two hours Seth Tikka Ram ate my brains up and I couldn't do any work at all. If you had been there I could have gone to the office for a while."

"Bhaiya, I don't have the energy to take Seth Tikka Ram's nonsense," Puran said, making a face.

"Nevertheless, you had better come outside."

"There, that serves him right," smiling, Lata whispered under her breath.

On his way out Puran bumped into Chamki. She looked upset and angry. Puran reached out and pinched her in the ribs. She felt cleansed, she was shining again, but not with anger.

Flowers

"The dining room, the veranda, Bhabi and Bare Bhaiya's bedroom and…"

"And what about me?"

Startled, Asha turned and saw Puran chewing on a match. She had been counting vases.

"You're not putting any flowers in my room."

"But Chamki is the one who puts flowers there…"

"That Chamki again! So what if she puts flowers there. You are arranging flowers in every other room except mine, I'm going to lodge a complaint."

"I'll take a vase to your room, too…" Asha quickly began sifting through the remaining flowers.

"No, not these dead white flowers that look like they belong on a corpse. I want those red ones."

So Asha took the red flowers to his room and arranged them in a vase. But all the while her heart thumped violently, as if she were stealing. Unless it was absolutely necessary she never stepped into Puran's room. What if Chamki appeared without notice?

During dinner Puran thanked her quietly for the flowers and she ran from there with the food tray in her hands. Later in the afternoon, when she happened by the veranda on the way to her room, she felt as if someone had kicked her; scattered about near the drain were the red flowers. She hastened to her room.

'This is the punishment for your boldness,' she scolded herself, lying on the floor as if some earthshaking event had taken place. Humiliation, anger at herself, and a host of strange feelings invaded her thoughts and left her troubled and depressed. They had wilted, who knows how long they had been lying near the drain and how they must have suffered the cold, she thought. All at once the sound of whistling startled her. Usually, because of all the work she had to do, she did not have time to see who was doing what, but from her place on the floor in her room where no one ever came except herself, she could peek at him through the chink in the door. What was that smiling, mischievous face like? She saw it a hundred times during the day, but she couldn't recall a single feature. Why? The reason was that she had never really looked at him closely.

She saw a pair of large, fair-skinned feet encased in sandals and topped by striped pyjamas abruptly come to a halt near the flowers. Asha held her breath. Two hands were lowered and the flowers were swept up. Asha's eyes closed and she clung to the earth on which she lay as though she wanted to be swallowed by it; after all this was the earth that had given birth to those red flowers.

"Who threw these fresh flowers here? This isn't a public garden," a voice said and the sandals disappeared.

For a long time Asha remained prostrate on the floor with her forehead glued to the earth.

In the evening when she was returning from a walk with Chota Munna in his carriage, Puran came up and started kissing the baby.

"Munna, oh Munna! I feel like swallowing up your cheeks, and you're so naughty, pretending to be so quiet, I know you well now. All this talk of work, work, work. I wish Bhagwan would take work out of this world. Why don't you ever talk to anyone?'

Asha, twisting the knob on the handle of the baby's carriage, stood quietly nearby.

Puran continued, "I know what it is, you think I'm not a very nice person, I'm an orge, I'll devour you."

Puran lifted his face and looked at Asha. She was frightened by the intensity of his gaze. "You think I'm a lion, I will tear you into pieces and swallow you?" He continued looking at Asha. "And who knows, if that's what you really wanted, I could indeed devour you this very minute." Asha's discomfort made his heart melt and he bent over the baby again.

"And, Munna, do you know that I picked up those flowers? Chamki's a wretch, isn't she? Yes, she is. Those beautiful red flowers, red just like Munna's cheeks, I've stashed them safely in my drawer. Well, you must have a lot of work to do, right? You may leave now, yes, please go."

When Asha went past the bush with the red flowers she felt they were smiling quietly, smiling with their eyes shut.

Holi

The weather never ceases to toy with humans. In summer you feel like jumping into a sea of ice, and if someone speaks to you, you can do little more than snap back in response. Scorching heat, a dull ache, and without a fan, the feeling that you're simmering slowly. And if the fan is turned on, your head swims. Oh God! And winter? Lethargy, lassitude, cold, cold, everything so cold. Even the heart turns cold. When spring arrives, everything blooms, all that has been lying dormant, stirs. For no reason at all you feel mischievous and playful, tickled by a strange restlessness. And then comes Holi and it's as if a volcano has erupted. If Holi didn't come around every year, this heart would break out of its cage in frenzied madness. How long can a river be held back by a dam? Only so long as the dam can hold. But why hold back in the first place? On the day of Holi Asha's spirits danced, too. Bhabi had been tormented all morning; she was like a little nugget of coloured powder. Already she had changed her sari thrice. It seemed as if the colour from the powder had penetrated her very skin. What does vermilion do? Does it contain some secret ingredient which affects you like alcohol? The more it is rubbed on the more delirious you become.

Today even Bare Bhaiya was not spared. His turn came after Bhabi's. Asha emptied bucket after bucket over him and also splattered him with vermilion powder. As for herself, so far she had managed to slip out of everyone's hands like a slithery snake. Puran, meanwhile, had succeeded in creating havoc. When Bhabi finally fell down in exhaustion, he turned his attention to Bhola's aunt.

"You bully, why do you lock horns with me?" she roared in her manly voice.

"Dear Bhola's aunt, we are fated to be together. In my past life you must have belonged to me, why else…"

Her shrivelled hair glittered and bloomed with vermilion-coloured flowers, while suggestive, full-bodied invectives rang out as further embellishment.

"Hey, Puran, here's Asha," Bare Bhaiya said, trying to get rid of Asha, "let's see if you can cope with her."

Everyone egged Asha on. She became nervous. Puran advanced towards her in all his glory.

She succeeded in emptying a glass of coloured water over him, but hesitated when it came to the vermilion powder. If her face hadn't been covered with dye you would have seen that her skin was glowing with the brilliance of stars.

Puran was not about to drag his feet. He left her helpless. Her vision was blurred from all the coloured water on her face and the ground under her feet was wet and slippery; suddenly she lost her balance and fell from the veranda.

"You'll kill her, Puran, you wretch!" Bhabi pounced on him like an eagle.

"Look at this swelling on the poor girl's foot," Bhabi said as she lovingly warmed Asha's ankle with cotton. At the same time she continued to reprimand Puran. "You're always losing control, aren't you?"

"Come, Bhabi, that's enough." Puran sat down beside her and began heating cotton for Asha's ankle.

"You should be ashamed of yourself. Do you realise what a hulk you are and how tiny this poor girl is? If you had been playing Holi with Mahesh instead, he'd have shown you a thing or two." Bhabi thought highly of her brother Mahesh.

"But, Bhabi, did you ever hear of men playing Holi with other men? Why would I be playing with Mahesh?"

"Well, you can only pull your weight with this helpless girl then, right?"

"You know, Bhabi, this is what you should do."

Bhabi became attentive.

"Take a knife and run it across my throat, all right?"

"Hai, Ram! But..."

One of the children started crying just then and Bhabi dashed off to see who it was. Puran continued to heat the cotton pads.

"You made Bhabi scold me," Puran said, applying the cotton pad to Asha's ankle. Asha tried to wrestle the pad away from his hands.

"Let me do this, you want Bhabi to scold me again?"

But Asha covered her foot with both hands. "I'm all right now."

"Well, well, that was certainly quick."

"Yes," Asha answered hastily.

"Look...listen..." He felt helpless. "I'm going to tell Bhabi..."

"What will you tell her?" Asha said nervously. Her heart grew sick with guilt.

"I'll tell her, I'll tell her that…"

Asha stared at his face in apprehension.

"That's better." He placed the cotton pad on her ankle again. "Here's what happened, you know…" He distracted her with small talk. Holding her breath, Asha listened intently as if he were about to reveal some terrible secret of hers.

"Listen, I'll tell Bhabi, I mean I'll say, that is, if you hadn't let me warm your ankle properly, I would have told her."

"What?" Asha said in an expectant tone.

"I would have said, 'Asha hates me'."

Bhabi returned. Asha rubbed her ankle fearfully. How that wound hurt! Hate? Asha had never learned to hate anyone. And Puran? Hate Puran?

Hide-and-seek

Puran wasn't the child Bhabi said he pretended to be. Of course he had always been treated as a child and was spoilt, and his mischievous pranks added to the childish demeanour he presented; he did go around the house clowning with the servants and the kids, often encouraging them to climb all over the furniture with no thought to their grimy clothes and soiled feet. Sometimes, the racket he created made Bhabi's head swim so that she would run after the children with a stick.

In two days Kamlaji was arriving at her father's house. Bhabi had turned everything upside down in preparation for her sister-in-law's arrival. The house had become a nuisance for Puran. There was cleaning going on everywhere; he felt stifled. His own room had also been taken over by Bhabi. Kamlaji's husband was coming with her as well, a prospect that made Mataji very nervous; he was a well-endowed landowner and then, of course, he was a son-in-law. But in addition to that there was a possibility that their connection with his family might grow; his younger sister, Shanta, was still unwed and Puran had also reached a marriageable age.

At one point Puran came into the drawing-room with the children in tow and a game of hide-and-seek commenced. Poor Asha wandered in to do some dusting and found the place in an uproar.

"Please leave the room, I'm going to do some cleaning here," she said in a matter-of-fact tone.

"So this room is going to be cleaned, too!" Puran exclaimed.

"Yes," Asha replied softly and began moving the chairs.

"What is this? All the rooms are being cleaned. No, no cleaning here; we're playing hide-and-seek. Why don't you join us, Asha?"

"Yes, yes…" the children clung to her.

"Oh yes, she'll play. She'll be the dai."

"No, please, I can't, I don't know how…"

But Puran took hold of her and pushed her into a chair. "All right, we'll start now. I'll be the thief." He sat down on the floor at Asha's feet and rested his head against her knees. "Now cover my eyes properly," he said.

"No, please, Bhabi said…"

"She didn't say anything. Now make sure my eyes are covered, quickly." He took a corner of her sari and placed it over his eyes.

"Chacha, no cheating." Nirmal was, after all, a businessman's son.

"It's your Ashaji who's cheating. Here, cover my eyes tightly, like this." He took Asha's hands and placed them over his eyes.

Asha became nervous. But the children hid and the game began.

"This is not fair." Asha tried to pull her hands away from Puran's face.

"Why, yes, I'm going to eat you up, aren't I? Why are you so afraid of me? I won't rest until I drive out this fear, Asha Devi—understand? Have I ever hurt you that you should be so afraid of me? Hunh? You chat with Bhaiya, have long talks with Bhabi, you even engage in such friendly chatter with Bhola's aunt. I'm the only one—tell me, why?" His eyes, in complete disregard of the rules of the game, were open. Asha was overwrought.

"Chote Bhaiya, please...all right, I'll clean the room later; you continue playing."

"I am playing." Puran looked more serious than Bare Bhaiya ever could. "You think I'm always playing games, don't you? All this is a game, my life, everything I say—you think all this is a game, don't you, Asha? You think I'm playing a game with you, too. How can I convince you I'm not?"

"Come and find us!" one of the children yelled.

"It's not a game, Asha, listen..." he chewed his lips helplessly.

"Come and find us!" Nirmal called in an impatient voice. He was tired of crouching behind the sofa.

"Please don't think of any of this as a game, Asha...for Pramatma's sake. You think I'm a child? If you hate me, tell me and I'll accept it. All right, now I know, you do hate me."

Asha had been sitting despondently with her head lowered. She glanced furtively at Puran. She was no child. Yes, unfortunately she was not a child. She had understood everything well, and not just what was happening today; for many days now she had felt the truth shake her soul.

"Bhabi will be coming here any minute," she said, trying to move Puran's head away from her knees.

"Chacha, you're not coming to look for us...we're not playing anymore." Sheela grumbled from her hiding place.

"Just answer my question, do you hate me?"

For a while Asha couldn't summon up the courage to lift her head and face Puran; she couldn't bear to look into his eyes. Finally she mustered some strength, raised her head and gave her answer with one look. Then hastily, she lowered her head again and covered her face with her hands.

"Asha!" Bhabi was calling her.

Dazed, Puran sat as if trying to seize a dream. The seriousness that had haunted his face earlier was gone; for a split second he paused, then a river of joy and emotion gushed forth, he shouted, "Coming to get you!" and went after the kids. Asha pretended to busy herself with straightening things near the fireplace. She crouched low on the carpet fearfully, her eyes closed, as if feeling around for some lost object. She wished she could sink into the ground, deep into the bowels of the earth under her feet.

"What is this!" Bhabi screamed, her voice barely discernible over the din Puran and the children were making.

"Hide-and-seek, Bhabi!" Puran said joyfully, speaking like someone intoxicated. "Come and join us."

"A curse upon hide-and-seek! Asha, you call this cleaning?"

"Bhabi, we've been playing hide-and-seek, and Ashaji was playing with us. Come, Bhabi, you'll be the dai now." Puran lifted Bhabi in his arms and twirled her around.

"Puran, Hai Ram! Puran! Put me down!" The children forgotten, Bhabi tried to extricate herself from Puran's ticklish grasp.

Sister-in-law

Devar, the word is as lively as sister-in-law, devrani, is dull. Until the devrani comes along, the bhabi is the queen of the household and the centre of interest for the devar. But as soon as the devrani arrives on the scene the devar disappears. No longer whispering everything in Bhabi's ears, he now quietly listens instead to his queen's complaints about Bhabi, and slowly turns into a poisoned thorn. The very same Bhabi without whom a meal tastes bitter, who can be teased and then pacified by putting one's arms around her neck, must contend with just "Namaste, Bhabiji" after the arrival of the queen.

"There will be two of us then and more trouble than you can dream of," Puran said when Bhabi brought up the question of his marriage.

"Hunh! You could be two or four, it doesn't really matter. I'll give you both a thrashing when I see fit."

"But, Bhabi, you'll hit her? Won't you feel sorry for her?"

"She'll be punished if she's mischievous."

"But what if she is very innocent?" Puran cast a glance at Asha who was sitting some distance away on the grass with Munna.

"I hope Bhagwan will not give you a wife who is innocent. You won't let her live."

"Bhabi, what a thing to say! Do all of you think I'm a dog?"

"Anyway, we're searching for someone very pretty."

"Searching? How long will you search? At this rate you'll find someone when I'm an old man."

"Actually, there is someone…and she's beautiful…"

"Is that true? Well, I have someone in mind, too, and she's also very beautiful." Asha was attempting to hide behind Munna. If she had had a choice she would have run from there.

"Liar! You couldn't have seen her. Have you seen Kamla's sister-in-law?"

"No, I haven't seen Kamla's sister-in-law, but I've seen a kamal." Puran's gaze sought Asha's eyes, but she was looking down at the grass as if in search of a hole she could disappear into.

"Is Shanta coming as well?" Bare Bhaiya, who was sitting in an armchair nearby reading a newspaper, asked.

"No, she's not coming. But you've seen her, haven't you?"

"Yes, but she was very young at the time. I think she was in F.A."

"That's right." Bhabi's attention wandered to Munna who had crawled away from Asha. Just as Asha got up to leave Bhabi called her.

"Asha, will you take Munna?"

Munna stiffened when Asha tried to hold him in her arms and, freeing himself, climbed over Puran.

"You see, Bhabi, the more I tease him the more he laughs," Puran said.

"It's your doing that he's so shameless."

"Bhabi, find a devrani who resembles Munna." It seemed Puran found the word vastly amusing.

"Oh no! You mean like this little monkey?"

"Well, someone who looks like you then. Petite, delicate. Tell me, Bhabi, why is it that you have several vagabond brothers but not even one sister?"

Bhabi remembered her only sister who had died of smallpox as a child. Had she lived she would have made the best sister-in-law. Bhabi began talking about her, how she crawled, how she lisped when she talked, and how the two of them quarrelled.

"Bhabi, for goodness sake, of what use would a little lisping wife be?"

"Don't be silly, Puran, she wouldn't still be lisping. And she would have been twelve or thirteen years old now."

"No, this won't do. Why must Bare Bhaiya have such a nice wife? He's always been ahead of me. He came into the world first, and he also managed to find a nice wife first. Why couldn't I have been born before him?"

"Enough silliness, Puran," Bhabi was blushing and Bare Bhaiya, hearing his wife's praise, smiled sheepishly. Puran had such a habit of blabbing nonsense.

"No!" Puran yelled. Munna had taken out his pen and was pushing it into the ground. There was ink all over his face.

"Dear me! No wonder he was so quiet all this time."

"You bad boy!" Puran pinched Munna's cheeks and catching hold of his chubby legs, pulled him.

"Leave my child alone, Puran—"

"I'll kill him today, Bhabi—that was a twenty-one rupee pen."

"You can take his father's pen—he has two."

"I'm not taking anyone's father's pen. I'll teach him a lesson today." Puran sat him on his knees. "You little devil!" The little devil smacked Puran across the face with an ink-stained hand.

Bhabi rolled on the grass, helpless with laughter.

"Why are you laughing? You just wait and see what I do to him." Puran lifted the child up and flung him in the air. Then, turning him upside down, he swung him about.

"Oh no! Puran! My baby, oh, his intestines are going to turn over, oh my poor baby." Bhabi was about to cry, but Munna, his face smeared with ink, continued to giggle. And when Bhabi tried to take him from Puran, he clung to Puran's shoulder and wouldn't let go.

"What a stubborn one he is," his father said.

"He is not going to learn like this." Puran grabbed the baby's cheek and twisted it. Munna's face began to crumple, Bhabi screamed, and Asha snatched Munna away.

"You just wait, Puran. I promise I'll treat your children the same way—actually, they'll get worse from me."

"No, you won't. My children won't be nobodies."

"And mine are?"

"Maybe not. But you won't be able to beat my children."

"Oh? And you can beat mine all you want?"

"There will be someone to protect them—you won't be able to touch them. If your children can be protected, mine will be protected, too."

"Hunh! No one will be able to protect your children from my wrath. You've thrashed my children so much I'll—"

"No, you won't. Munna will protect them, or someone else will. Asha, you'll protect them, won't you?"

Asha busied herself with tying Munna's shoelaces.

The Fair

Asha had been living at Raja Sahib's for a whole year, and in all this time there had been no reason for her to return to her village. But the village fair came along and Ranji's mother thought of Asha. Ranji borrowed some money, had a new suit of clothes made for himself, and both mother and son arrived at Raja Sahib's. Asha was reluctant to return with them alone, so Ranji's mother coaxed Chamki into going along and the four embarked on the trek back to the village. On the way Ranji's mother stopped to chat with somebody and was left behind. Ranji took charge of Asha and Chamki and continued on.

The importance of the fair was evident from the way people thronged the roads. A colourful array of dupattas, turbans and caps adorned the streets; trooping along hurriedly were hundreds of vendors carrying toy paper fans and birds slung on long bamboo poles; also advancing towards the site of the fair were carts laden with gazak, chaat, and sweets fried in oil, accompanied by the buzz of flies; merchants carrying colourful hair ribbons and beaded necklaces hurried along with the vendors; and adding to the festivities was a tumult of lost donkeys, sick cows and mangy dogs. All in all, it seemed that heaven had arrived on earth with the fair for a couple of days.

In addition to the decorative shops constructed with bamboo and coloured paper, there were expensive goods of all shapes and sizes strewn about in great number on the fair grounds. Among these were Japanese toys, clay idols, rubber balloons and bamboo reeds, which the vendors played to attract the public. One could also see a bear, a five-legged cow, a two-headed calf's cadaver, a fox with a man's face, a magician, and jugglers who jumped from bamboo poles with far greater alacrity than monkeys.

And in the midst of all this, Ranji was treating the girls to all these delights in grand style; already they had had potato chaat, dahi-bare and papri. The purple-edged turban glowed against Ranji's dark skin, the edges of his striped yellow shirt billowed with the wind revealing his charming pink underwear under his diaphanous dhoti. New plaid socks, held up with red rubber bands on his stocky, hairy calves looked quite jaunty, and the large gilt rings on his fingers, together with the red Japanese silk handkerchief, were enough to wrench one's heart. Kallo, the sweeperess, sneaked coquettish glances at him, Roopa's widowed daughter-in-law blushed when he ran into her, and a few of his friends teased him with profanities, but Ranji was in very high society at the moment; rolling his eyes, pulling in his pot belly, he moved on.

Asha, who had not only never been to the fair before but who, in her grandmother's lifetime, had not even ventured to the shop down the street to buy oil, was bewildered by the crowds and the strange goings-on. She kept colliding into people, and every once in a while she was jostled or pushed by someone behind her. And when she glimpsed Puran in a hat, riding his chestnut mare in the midst of all this pushing and shoving, she nearly fell on her face. Suddenly, she wanted to hide. However, suffused with the importance of his position as a landowner, Puran rode past her haughtily without noticing her. Asha breathed a sigh of relief.

But moments later, while she was haggling over the price

of bracelets made from melon seeds, Puran rode over to her side. Perhaps he had seen her, after all. But why wasn't he smiling if he had? Abandoning the bracelets, she hastily made her way through the crowds, but no crowd could forestall the stride of the chestnut mare. Not when she was watching the puppet show, nor when she was looking at some colourful ribbons later, nor even when she was gulping down a soda drink. And to make matters worse, just as she was demurring at Ranji's offer of a silver-coated paan, the mare seemed to hover over her. And the rider? He was still on the horse, but his eyebrows curved angrily and his face had turned red. The paan fell from Asha's hand and landed on the ground, its mouth split open. Well, there would be other paans; this wasn't real silver anyway, perhaps gilt or some such thing. And the worst of it was that Chamki was nowhere in sight. A minute ago she had been counting bangles with Lakshmi, and the next minute she had flown!

"Let's go home now. Where's Chamki?" Asha said, trying to repress an unknown fear that kept growing.

"So soon? There's plenty of daylight left," Ranji said, although dusk had already settled in the east. Today Ranji, feeling courageous, walked with an air of resolution. He exhibited a new image. Paan after paan had been consumed and he had successfully reduced several packets of biris to ashes. His gait was becoming more and more languid and the smoke from the biris darkened.

"Where is Chamki? Why didn't she tell me she was going off somewhere?"

"She's probably with Lakshmi. Let's go and see the wrestling match."

"No," Asha said, shaking her head vehemently. What a thing to see! Masses of naked flesh rolling about in the dust while the spectators, all good-for-nothing vagabonds, swore and offered revolting suggestions to the wrestlers. Asha shuddered at the very thought, and was shocked when she caught a glimpse of the inky-black, naked limbs of the wrestlers from afar.

"All right, let's go and have some sherbat then. We'll find Chamki. What are you scared of?" Ranji drew closer to Asha.

At the sherbat-wallah's Asha came face to face with a scene that robbed her of her equilibrium altogether. The men who were drinking sherbat loitered in the area of the shop with frightening expressions on their faces, while others rolled about in the dirt. A gramophone nearby blared away. No sooner had these two arrived than the men began ogling her with phlegm-coloured eyes. As if this were not enough, they proceeded to exchange obscenities accompanied by vulgar gestures. And then there was the smoke from the biris and the rank odour of the sherbat itself. Asha felt nauseated.

"Let's go," she pleaded tearfully. She had also glimpsed the chestnut steed and its rider. "Let's go this minute," she said and moved away from Ranji.

"Where are you going? Wait, I'll come with you." Ranji was intimidated by Asha and the obscenities were making him nervous. Also, a red-turbaned policeman had been eyeing him suspiciously for a long time.

"Wait here. I'll see if I can find Chamki." Ranji simply wanted to escape for a while so he could gather his wits. He knew Chamki wasn't lost and would come looking for them when she was ready.

Asha leaned against a bamboo jalousie and tried to still her wildly beating heart.

"So, this is what you have been up to."

Startled, Asha jumped aside; she could have been trampled by the horse if she hadn't moved so quickly.

"Who is the scoundrel with you?" Decency and jealousy don't go hand in hand, but Puran wasn't one to think before he spoke.

"Ranji," Asha murmured, picking at a splinter in the bamboo.

"Ranji—the name's certainly beautiful. I didn't know you were interested in the sherbat."

Had she even glanced at the sherbat? And what kind of sherbat was it that smelled like dog's vomit!

"Who gave you permission to come here by yourself?"

"Chamki—is here with me, too."

"But why did you come? And aren't you ashamed to be seen chewing paan and drinking tarhi?" Puran spoke in a controlled voice.

It seemed that if he could have, he would have taken the whip which he was striking at the bamboo rods in the jalousie, and skinned her with it. Asha wished he would, instead of speaking to her in this manner. She didn't know how to respond.

"You can do what you want, but remember everyone knows you are a servant in our household. Pitaji will get a bad name."

Asha was amazed that Puran should talk to her like this. Yes, indeed she was his servant, only a servant. Suddenly she was filled with a desire to scrape her hands against the bamboo rods till they bled or tear her heart out and sob unashamedly. How long had she carried a burden in her heart.

"And how innocent you seemed. One little question and you started quivering and shaking as if you were a little girl! I didn't know you at all!" Puran chewed his words, flinging them at her like stones, and her fear grew. The mare was stomping restlessly, and all the while the whip kept striking at the bamboo rods.

Suddenly the mare bucked and Puran dug his heels into her sides with full force. She reared, missing Asha by inches, and then galloped off. The chestnut mare was also punishing her.

Asha couldn't stay there any longer. The ruffians loitered around her, first coughing knowingly, then humming lines from film songs. She was so terrified she wanted to run from there. A few men, standing not far from her, lazily scratched their thighs and eyed her with syrupy looks. They had all fallen madly in love with her, it seemed. Walking away, making her way through the throng of men, she found herself next to a pole. Distressed, she stopped and looked around frantically.

Standing in the midst of friends, not too far from her, was Chamki. She giggled bashfully while saying something to the suave rider of the horse whose eyes were concealed under the rim of the hat, but whose lips, Asha could see, quivered in a naughty smile.

"Don't you want to see the fireworks?" Chamki said, surprised at Asha's insistence on leaving in such a hurry. "The fireworks are the best part of the fair. And Chote Bhaiya is here too, did you see him? He's so wicked!" Holding back a laugh, Chamki puckered her lips.

"Right in front of everyone he said, 'Chamki, will you sit on the horse, you must be tired.' Hunh!"

But Chamki didn't see too much of the fireworks. There were fireworks going off in her own heart.

An anar thundered; a glittering gold cloud rose and there was light everywhere, then darkness. A fire-cracker went off, illuminating the very depths of being, and finally total, absolute darkness! How dull life appears afterwards, like the empty clay shell of a spent anar or the tail of a fire-cracker!

Hatred

When, tired and exhausted, Asha returned from the fair to her room, her body ached like a ripe sore. As she poured water over the blisters on the soles of her feet to wash off the mud, her muscles contracted sharply with pain and she broke out in a sweat. But what of the larger sores that mushroomed in her heart and in her mind? She wished everyone would fall asleep so that she could hide her face in her pillow and sob without restraint. Her temples pounded with the weight of emotions she had stifled, her forehead throbbed. The body is weak, but why was her heart so timorous? Her grandmother used to say it was because she had been a premature baby, but how was that her fault? She was in no hurry to come into the world; if her young brother had not slipped and fallen she would not have come at the appointed time.

During mealtimes she noticed that Puran neither teased Bhabi nor did he pinch the children's cheeks, and she didn't catch him laughing in his usual manner either.

"Oh my! How quiet you are today," Bhabi said. But God knows what held Puran's attention. Bhabi mischievously put a spoonful of salt in his soup and shook his shoulder.

"Are you asleep? The food won't be left here for you all night."

Puran began gulping down the soup. "All right Bhabi, one day soon it will be my turn." They were all laughing at him; Puran's discomfort became evident. Chamki gave him a fresh plate of soup and he pretended to be engrossed in eating. But things were not right today; Puran neither ate properly nor would he talk. When Asha served him his favourite dal, he said, "I don't want any." Actually he might have had some, but as soon as he saw Asha he looked away irately, and busied himself instead with the papads Chamki was serving. Scared, Asha moved away quickly.

"Puran, how can you scold my Asha? Is that any way to speak to anyone?" Bhabi spoke angrily.

"Who am I to scold your Asha? I'm just not hungry, that's all. Excuse me." Puran rose from the table.

"But Puran, you haven't eaten anything." Bhabi looked worried.

"I don't feel very well." Puran left the table and went to his room.

Maybe it was just a coincidence or maybe it was the heat, but the next day Puran developed a high fever that left him floating in and out of consciousness for days. The fever persisted, occasionally subsiding just a little at a time, leaving Puran irritable and testy. Asha was afraid to go into his room, yet, as if propelled by some secret force, she would find herself at his door on one pretext or another. He had had a rough night and Bhabi was exhausted. When Asha went past the door she called out to her: "Asha, my doll, come and sit here for a while. I need to get some air, I'll be back in a few minutes."

Asha tiptoed in and sat down quietly on a stool near Puran's bed. It had been a long time since she had had the opportunity of looking at his face closely. How mature he looked, just like Raja Sahib. Two days of fever had left him pale, his lips were chapped and his hair tousled. Asha wanted to straighten every little lock, to move her fingers gently and lovingly on his forehead. Perhaps the soul is awake even when the body slumbers. Asha's scrutiny awoke Puran. He shut his eyes and opened them again and stared at her. She found his gaze disturbing. The fever had no doubt agitated his brain for he was flushed. All at once his eyes burned with life and his lips parted joyfully.

"Asha," he whispered, trying to lift himself on one elbow.

Asha got up hastily. She was at a loss, didn't know what to do. For a few minutes Puran continued to stare at her. Then his eyes fell on her wrist; he saw the bangles he had seen Ranji buy for her at the fair, and that necklace with the white beads. He fell back on his pillow as if someone had knocked his elbow. Asha rushed to his side but he was like a man possessed by a demon.

"Leave me alone...where is everybody?" he looked around the room frantically.

"Should I get Bhabi?" Asha turned towards to the door.

"Hai Bhagwan! Where is everyone! Is everyone dead? Where is Chamki?"

"Bhabi was very tired, and Chamki—shall I get her?"

"Bhabi got tired and left you here? Why did she trouble you? Is there no one else in the house?" Puran spoke in a cutting tone. "I'm so thirsty, and this darkness..." He began thrashing about feverishly.

Confused, not knowing whether to give him water or call Bhabi, Asha simply stood before him like an idiot. But she was such an idiot!

"Ohh...I can't breathe...it's so dark...pull the curtains away from the window..."

Asha ran to draw the curtains. It wasn't quite evening yet, but the room had darkened just a bit. Her hands trembled when she realised that Puran was still staring at her. When she reached for the curtain next to his bed she found herself close to his pillow; to avoid his searing gaze she bent over inches away from his face. The curtains fully drawn, she decided to get Bhabi, but when she looked at Puran she saw that his eyes were closed. She sat down again. After a short while Puran opened his eyes. She jumped from her seat.

"Shall I get Bhabi now?" she volunteered.

"Hunh! You can go if you don't feel like staying, I want to be alone. Where is Chamki? Why didn't Bhabi leave her here instead of you... please go."

"Chamki was also very tired. She's taking a...nap." Asha was holding back her tears with great difficulty. "Chamki is asleep, Bhabi is tired, you are tired, you can leave, I don't need anyone. Go."

The tears began to flow.

"There you go, crying now, what have I said to you? Who can say anything to you, you are free to go anywhere you want."

"Why...what are you saying... I..."

"What have I done now? Why don't you run to Bare Bhaiya and complain that I scolded you when I saw you with Ranji... I don't care, why should I care..."

"When did I complain to Bare Bhaiya?"

"So now you're lying also. Didn't you tell Bare Bhaiya that I was angry with you? Why would I be angry with you, why?"

"I didn't complain to Bare Bhaiya! He asked me, 'Is Puran angry with you?' I... I said, 'No', and then he said, 'Why is he, why is he like...'" Asha didn't know how to continue.

"All right, so you didn't say anything to him. But you're upset that I spoke to you so harshly. I shouldn't have said anything, I hope you will deign to forgive me." Puran's tone was caustic but he didn't sound angry any more.

"But I'm not upset," Asha made an attempt to be bold.

"Maybe not. But I'm sure you didn't like my interference in your affairs. Who am I...you can see Ranji whenever you want to. It's foolish of me to interfere, you have the right to do as you please." Puran smiled.

"You're...you're so cruel!" Asha burst into tears.

"I've heard that you are engaged to Ranji. It's my fault, Asha, I'm a fool. I scolded you for no reason at all. You like Ranji, don't you?"

Asha glared at Puran, making him break into a laugh. "And what about your...Chamki?" Asha mumbled between sobs.

"Chamki? What? My Chamki? Who says? Hush!" He tried to get up. "What a silly thing you are."

"I know everything," Asha said in a child's voice.

"But who told you that Chamki."

"And who told you that Ranji..."

"Asha." Puran gazed into her eyes. Her face was puffed up from weeping. "Asha, I'm a terrible person, my own dear Asha." He struggled to get out of bed.

"Please lie down," Asha tried to push him back.

"Asha, I'm so hasty, so hateful." He grasped her shoulders with both hands, but overcome with emotion and a wave of weakness, he tottered on his feet.

"What is this!" Bare Bhaiya, who came into the room just then, caught Puran in his arms. "What is this, Asha?"

What could Asha have done?

"Bhaiya, didn't you know better than to entrust someone as stubborn and unmanageable as me to Asha's care? How could she stop me?"

"You should have stopped him," Bhabi said. "Why didn't you call me?"

"Bhabi, my dear, do you think I would have listened to her? She tried her to best to stop me...Bhabi, some water, please..." Puran fainted.

Commotion swept up the entire household but Asha was vindicated. The doctor explained that Puran's sudden weakness was a good sign, a direct result of the fever subsiding, and after a few days of bed rest he would recover completely.

In the days that followed Puran turned into such a clown of a patient that it was nearly impossible to keep him confined to his bed. He wanted everyone in his room, even Bhola's aunt. And Asha, from whom Puran's eyes had sought forgiveness a hundred times, also sneaked in with the others.

"Bhola's aunt, if you get angry with me once for some reason, will you never make up with me?"

"Be quiet, you crazy boy."

"No, I mean it. If I upset you, do you make up your mind to hold a grudge against me for life?"

"What?" Bhola's aunt had no idea what he was talking about.

"Bhola's aunt, look, we all make mistakes, don't we?"

"Who made a mistake?" she asked foolishly.

"You're so dense...how will we spend our life together?"

"Spend your life with your mother and sister!"

"If you are Bhola's aunt, what will my relationship to Bhola be?"

Bhola's aunt proceeded to describe a relationship so disgusting that Puran was forced to hide his face in his blanket. How could such a patient keep still in bed for long?

This was the hatred that had burst like a storm in Puran's heart and in two swift jolts had weakened him to the bone. But now it was the same again. How does one develop such violent hatred and then poof! it evaporates like steam. He had decided this was it, the game was over. And within minutes he was clean, like the smooth surface of a clay water-pot. Good grief! Is this hatred? It is just another fanciful aspect of love.

The old pranks returned, the taunting attacks on Bhabi, Bhola's aunt's profanities. Asha's hide-and-seek, and the teasing of the children. Why do you become so light-headed when you're in love? Why do the body and the eyes dance with merriment as does the heart? And why does everything seem to be made for the purpose of gaiety? Where does sobriety take off to? And you have no thought of tomorrow. But a woman? How cautious she is. Her heart quivers fearfully all the time, if she laughs it is with trepidation, if she smiles she does so hesitatingly. At every step she is afraid her secret will be revealed. What will happen? How will it happen? And what if this comes about, or that? And then, the unfortunate creature also considers herself a fool.

Asha had just given Munna a bath and was now combing his hair. He twisted and turned and wouldn't sit still at all, tossing a box here, opening a bottle there, chewing on the comb, turning the surma-dani upside down. Asha was getting annoyed.

"You bad boy!" she said, snatching the surma pin from him.

"Who? Me?" Puran spoke in a frightened child's voice from the door.

"No, it's Munna, he won't let me comb his hair."

"Munna's very naughty, he's not scared of you, you're such a chicken yourself…frightened off by a little baby frog!"

That morning Puran had surprised Bhabi with a tiny frog perhaps the size of a berry. Bhabi ran crazily all over the house.

"This won't do, Puran, tie it to a string and hang it around her neck." Instead of coming to her rescue her husband was offering suggestions on how to destroy her.

"Puran, my dearest brother, I beg you, on my life…" Bhabi was screaming now. Turning away from Bhabi, Puran threw the frog on Asha who had been watching this drama in amusement all this time. Asha fled from there as though she were being pursued by a lion. And when Puran slipped a fragment of paper in her lap, she began pulling and tugging nervously at a corner of her dhoti.

"Would it have devoured you, that tiny frog?"

"Frogs make me sick."

"But why did you run from the garden? Do I make you sick as well?" Puran took the brush from her hands.

Asha picked up another brush and continued combing Munna's hair.

"What is this, Asha devi?" Puran snatched the other brush from her.

"I had things to do."

"That's right, you have the whole world to take care of." Using both brushes Puran set to combing his hair.

"Raja Sahib must be home now, he'll be looking for you."

"There you go again, thinking of everyone else except me, and if I tell you to do something you start making one excuse after another. Just think, Asha."

Asha picked up Munna and made as if to leave.

"So, running away again," Puran said, grasping her hands with both of his.

"Let me go, Munna is hungry."

"Who is holding you, I'm kissing Munna…why, shouldn't I kiss Munna? Hunh?" And he began kissing Munna. Asha turned her face this way and that but Puran's hair covered her eyes and her cheeks, then her heart and her head.

"Puran, I wish you had time for more important things." It was Bare Bhaiya. "Come with me."

"Me? I'm coming." And Puran followed him out of the room.

Asha breathed a sigh of relief and rested her face against Munna's cheeks.

~

"I don't like this at all, I don't approve of your behaviour," Bare Bhaiya said in a serious tone.

"My...what...who?"

"Yes, your behaviour. I'm not blind, Puran Singh. This constant joking with the girls..."

"What jokes, Bare Bhaiya, I don't joke with them. As for Asha, I feel sorry for her, after all she's the granddaughter of our wet nurse, actually Grandfather's wet nurse."

"But your teasing is in very bad taste."

"Bhaiya...you don't understand...you're mistaken, I don't feel sorry for Asha...I love her and..."

"And? And? And nothing! Puran, have you ever known me to glance at any of the female servants? We are true princes, our honour does not permit such actions."

"But I want to marry her."

"You?" Bhaiya laughed derisively.

"Why do you laugh?"

"Because you won't marry her."

"How can you say that, Bhaiya?"

"I can, that's all. I don't make jokes, I don't have the time to laugh all day long, and this notion you have of marriage—some idea!"

"But why do you object? I'd like to know." Puran twisted the ends of his shirt front nervously.

"She's our servant, Puran. You are probably thinking these foolish thoughts because of some film you've seen. But you should be aware that life is not a film, life is reality, a very real reality, and you are not a child."

"I know I'm not a child, and that is why I must know why I can't do as I please."

"Yes, but who gave you the right to dishonour your family and break the hearts of your elders?"

"The family, hunh! The same old story. I know that Pitaji is not that old-fashioned."

"That's where you're wrong, you are mistaken. No matter how enlightened Pitaji is, he will never give you permission for such a horrible undertaking, and just think, what has Mataji or the children, your innocent nephews and nieces, what have they done to deserve being sacrificed?"

"What are you talking about? What sacrifice?"

"What place will they hold in society after this? Well, Uncle Puran married a servant girl. What decent family is going to ask for Sheela's hand in marriage, and what family will give Nirmal their daughter after his uncle's actions become public knowledge?"

"To hell with such society, with people who will reproach Sheela because her uncle married a girl from a poor family. It will be better for Sheela to remain unmarried rather than be married to someone with such despicable ideas."

"Of course. It's easy for you to say all this, to make plans for your own happiness while the rest of the family is destroyed."

"That's not true! All I'm saying is we won't marry our Sheela into a family which subscribes to such old-fashioned views."

"So you believe that I should look for someone related to Asha, a custodian, or a steward, for Sheela?" Bare Bhaiya was not a very talkative man, he wasn't stupid. Puran felt helpless in the face of his taunts.

"You're misconstruing everything I'm saying, Bhaiya," Puran said, defeated.

"Think well, you're wiser and more intelligent than I am. Anyway, let's drop the subject for the moment, your Bhabi is coming this way. I don't want this matter made known until it's absolutely necessary."

Bhabi arrived with her kids in tow.

"Look, did you see how Munna kisses my cheek?" Munna squeezed his mother's face with his short, stubby fingers and placed his flat nose on her cheek.

"He learns from copying," Bare Bhaiya hinted obliquely and Puran tried to conceal his embarrassment by turning to his usual pranks with Munna.

"Bhabi, I'm going to make him stand, he's old enough to learn now." Puran put Munna down.

"Hey, Ram! No, Puran, no! He's too young to stand by himself yet."

"I don't care, he can do it, he's so fat, surely he can stand, he's just pretending he can't."

"I don't see how a ten-month-old baby can pretend, he just can't do it, that's all." Bhabi tried to wrest Munna away from Puran.

"I don't care, I'm going to let go of his hands." Puran wanted to frighten her.

"Oh, my baby! Puran!" She snatched Munna out of Puran's grasp.

"What are you worried about? Did you really think I'd let go of his hands? I'm not his enemy." With these words Bare Bhaiya's remarks echoed in Puran's ears.

The Blow

There is only one way life ends, with death. But we forget that every morning ends with night, slumber with waking, and laughter with silence. The beauty of sunrise would have gone unnoticed if it hadn't been for sunset, if the sun straddled the sky forever. And may God keep us from a sleep from which there is no waking. But the blows God has deemed necessary for lovers are a shade too many. One kind of blow, related to the appearance of the rival, leaves you frustrated, but no sooner do the clouds dissipate than the moon appears again and all is well; a little bit of unhappiness, like a full stop after a sentence, makes life interesting. Then there is another kind of blow your friends and well-wishers make ready for you. This is the backlash from society. If you're lucky you might leap across the ditch, but if you're not, it's right there in front of you. You can recover from other kinds of blows, but not the one society deals out. How both literature and films have dragged society into the mud, but like a hungry lion it leaps up, ready to attack. Actually, this is all just a front for something else. The collision is not with society but with people, with those you care about. And who would suffer more in a situation like this than someone as adventurous and carefree as Puran? Surely it couldn't be sombre, cautious Bare Bhaiya?

Puran's behaviour alerted the family members. Everyone's attention was trained like guns towards Puran and Asha. A change began to appear in the way Asha was treated. Instead of being placed with the other servant girls, she became a favourite of Mataji who coiled her presence around her like a snake. During meals she was made to sit beside Munna while Puran was seated between Mataji and Raja Sahib. Puran understood the reason for this close watch, but he had neither the courage nor the opportunity to get out from under. However, even if a thief can be prevented from stealing, he can't be forced to become honest. While leaning over Mataji's lap to get to Munna's cheeks, Puran did not refrain from sneaking a glance at Asha. And as if that was the reason for living, somewhere in the gallery, behind the drawing room curtains, you would find the honey hidden and the bees stuck to it in a stupor.

It was Munna's birthday. And Diwali was also just around the corner. The house was getting a thorough cleaning. Anyway, how long can flies buzz around for a kill? Asha was putting the curtains up in Bhabi's room. Puran arrived, pretending to be looking for something.

"I wish someone would tidy up and decorate my room as well," he said, standing close to her, one leg resting on a nearby chair.

"Your room is so sparse, what can one decorate it with?" Asha had learnt to talk back to Puran.

"Hunh! That's because I'm a poor man." His gaze travelled over Bhabi's silver things. "Bhabi's father is a millionaire."

"Don't lose heart, who knows, when you get married your wife will bring even more lavish things with her."

"I don't think so. What if my wife is poor?"

"Ram forbid that you have a poor wife."

"Why, is it a failing to be poor?"

"Of course. If it weren't a failing why would the upper class be so privileged?"

"But my wife-to-be *is* poor, she doesn't have money. She does have good looks, though."

"Oh my! But Chote Bhaiya, we'll be truly impressed if she has both money and good looks."

"I don't want money or good looks, I want..." Puran stammered. Asha continued to loop the curtains.

"Asha, is money everything? Suppose I lose everything, Pitaji doesn't give me a penny, will you, will you..."

Asha's hands trembled and the curtain rings slipped from her fingers and fell to the floor.

"Tell me, Asha, if I'm penniless and if Ranji..."

If only Ranji were dead, Asha thought. But she occupied herself with picking up the rings from the floor.

"And if Ranji has money, you won't think of me, will you?"

"What do you mean? Why should you become penniless?"

"Let's just say I do."

"Please don't talk like this," Asha pleaded.

"Why don't you take what I'm saying seriously, why don't you give me a proper answer? Hunh?"

"What can I say? You're going to be late for the match, you'll miss the train."

"Listen, I'm not joking and I don't have the time to listen to your excuses either. I've told you so many times how I feel and now I'm going to speak to Pitaji."

"No, please, for Pramatma's sake, don't do that."

"Why? Why shouldn't I tell him? What's the reason? He has often brought up the subject of my marriage."

"So why don't you marry?" Asha tried to change the subject.

"That's what I'm talking about. I'll tell him everything."

"No, please don't tell him anything. If you..."

"If I what? Go on. I'm going to inform him that I want to get married and that I don't need his money."

"No, you can't say that."

"Why not? Who will stop me?"

"I will stop you."

"What do you mean? You will say that…that…"

"Yes," Asha moved away from him quickly with the curtain.

"Asha, you're toying with my emotions. Why? Why are you doing this?" He caught hold of her arm.

"Because I want to."

"Because you want to? Don't you love me at all and…" He let go of her arm.

The curtains done, Asha started changing the slipcovers on the pillows.

"Say something, don't you love me? I'll never bother you again." He clasped her hand in his.

Asha tried to avoid his gaze. She could feel her eyes filling rapidly with tears.

"Just say once that you don't love me, that you don't love me as much I love you…speak, say something."

"No!" Asha exclaimed, unable to hold her emotions in check any longer.

Puran let go of her.

"Oh," he said with a laugh, "liar, what a liar you are. If I die, Asha…"

"That's enough," Asha interrupted him, "please leave now." She placed her hand on his mouth. "What can you get by teasing and taunting a poor woman like me? You and I are not suited to each other, you must be married to a princess."

"To hell with princesses, you're my princess. And who says we don't belong together? Look at that mirror, what does it say?"

Seeing herself so close to Puran, Asha forgot everything for a moment and rested her head on Puran's chest.

"I'll speak to Pitaji today, I don't care if he kills me," Puran began speaking softly in her ear, "and then, my dearest Asha…"

"Chamki!" Asha's eyes fell on the mirror and behind her she saw Chamki's face red with anger. Asha sprang away from Puran.

"Chamki? That witch is nothing. Are you still thinking of her, are you still jealous of the wretch?"

"No, she was here a moment ago."

"Oh, so she's spying on us. It doesn't matter, I don't care who else find out that I love Asha. I'm not afraid of anyone."

"Ah, such daring! Let me look at this valiant hero who's not afraid of anyone." Mataji's mighty presence loomed ominously in the doorway like a black cloud. At that moment Asha wished desperately she could turn into a fly, or turn to stone. As a matter of fact, she had already turned to stone.

"Mataji…"

"Silence! Aren't you ashamed, calling me Mata with the very lips with which you were licking filth from the gutter a moment ago?"

"But listen to me, please…"

"I've told you once to remain silent, Puran. I don't want to have anything to do with you. A person who has no regard for the honour of his family or his father's name can have no regard for his mother. It is this witch I must deal with." She moved towards Asha menacingly.

"But first you have to listen to me, then…"

"Tell me, you wretch, did we nurture four generations of your family so that you could poison us at the first chance you got? Speak, you ungrateful girl, answer me." She advanced. Asha's whole body quivered. In all this time Mataji had never cast a disapproving eye at her. Actually, she was not known to express disfavour with anyone. Her forceful personality and her air of authority were enough to strike fear into the hearts of those around her, and for the most part she stayed out of everyone's way, cloistered in her room, immersed in reading and worship. However, this was a matter of such immense import that she had been compelled to come down to earth from her heavenly domain.

"Asha, you are under my protection," Puran said, his heart wrenching at Asha's trembling.

"Oh? Let me see what kind of protection it is that you're offering. Puran Singh, you forget your place. Leave us. All I want to do is to ask this girl why she chose to repay our love and affection in this manner."

"Mataji, forgive me, please..." Asha fell at Mataji's feet.

"Forgiveness? You destroy my home and then ask for forgiveness? It's true, once you take in a low-class person, he will not be satisfied until he gets more and more from you. How did you even dare to do this?" When Mataji's anger was aroused she turned into Kali Ma. Taking hold of Asha's hair, she twisted her head back so that she was facing her.

"That's enough, Mataji, let her go." Puran pulled his mother away from Asha. "You're not listening at all."

"Puran, how can you do this?" Mataji's voice cracked. "What's all this wrangling about?" The wrangling had brought Raja Sahib out of his hole as well.

"Pitaji..."

"Do you see, do you see your beloved son's antics? Did you see how he twisted my wrist? Ahhh, Bhagwan!" Mataji caught her head in her hands and moaned threateningly.

"Puran, come outside." Faced with his mother's wrath, Bare Bhaiya also shook with fear. "But first ask for Mataji's forgiveness."

"Mataji ... I ... forgive me, but remember..."

Bare Bhaiya didn't allow him to continue. "That's enough nonsense, Puran." And he dragged him out of the room as if he were a child.

This, in reality, was the blow Puran received. And what happened in the course of this collision is what happens when a hammer comes down on glass. But once smashed, broken glass scatters and wounds the soles of all those who walk on it.

The Verdict

There is really no need to say this, but the verdict was issued. The whole family assembled. Mataji was in the judge's seat and Raja Sahib, assuming the role of a puppet, was also brought in. Who would be interested in such a dull affair; the heroine weeps alone in a dark chamber, the hero paces about in his room wearing the floor thin. And how else could such a hero and heroine fare? To top it all, the court was ready. When summoned, Puran came in with his face lowered, his hair awry. From behind the curtain Bhabi watched him in this condition and sighed. But could the sighs do anything to diminish anger?

"Come in, Puran. What is this dispute, son?" Pitaji had not fathomed the nature of the dispute as yet.

"There you go again, encouraging him. If you hadn't been so soft, these children might have been worth more today." Mataji knew, however, that her husband was a gem.

"All right, all right…yes, well, Puran, what's all this nonsense about? You had better return to college, enough preparation for the exam, I'd say."

"Pitaji, I'm not committing a sin."

"No," Mataji interjected, "this is no sin, it's an act of goodness, isn't it, smearing dirt on your family's name."

"Does one blacken one's name simply by getting married?"

"Marriage? You are not going to try and marry that low-caste wretch while I'm alive."

"Puran," Raja Sahib said in a conciliatory tone, "don't be so stubborn. Life is so short, why do you want to get into this? Let us suppose for a moment that you do marry that girl. Well, it will be a great mistake. Just think, do you imagine that your mother will let either you, me or that girl live in peace? Will she ever accept her?"

Mataji groaned. "I pray to Bhagwan I never have any kind of a relationship with her. Look here, ji, why are you beating about the bush, why don't you frankly say what you must say?"

"Because you won't let me get a word in. Now listen here, Puran, think carefully. How will she live here and then she, uh, she…" Raja Sahib liked to be thought of as a liberal. He hesitated.

"But Pitaji, you're a friend of harijans, how can you…"

"Harijans! It's these very harijans who have sunk our boat! You're not thinking, not reasoning. You had better return to your herbs and medicines, ji."

Poor Raja Sahib. Some years ago he had experimented with

drugs that are known to increase virility and strength. He found it embarrassing to be reminded of that episode in the presence of his grown sons.

"You're angry with Puran and you're taking that anger out on me. I'll say whatever you want me to, but nothing seems to make you happy."

"Look here, Puran," Bhaiya spoke up, "you understand the matter very clearly. I've told you this before. Try and think of how all this will affect our lives. What will Kamla's in-laws say, and what will my wife's family think, where will we hide our faces?"

"You're very selfish, Bhaiya. And what about your father-in-law? All his life he's lived on interest and now…"

Behind the curtain Bhabi trembled, then stepped back.

"Nevertheless, you will not be allowed to take this step."

"No one can make me do anything or stop me. I don't want anyone's help or interference. So Pitaji will deprive me of an income and I'll be penniless. Fine, I don't care about that at all."

Mataji retorted: "No, you don't care, but she whom you think of as a goddess, she will no doubt rush to marry you. Why, she won't even spit on you! Do you hear?"

"You don't understand her nor did you ever try to."

"I understand such base women well."

"That is enough, Mataji…Pitaji, Bhaiya, here's my answer. I will marry Asha and make the impossible possible. I'll leave this house today so that no one can blame you for anything."

"Wherever you go you'll be held responsible for disgracing your family's name. And people will say 'What a greedy old man, and all because the girl was poor'."

"People are crazy, you know."

"So? Is there no way out for me?"

"No, you were born here and—"

"I wish I had been born in a poor man's house, then no one would have taunted me. But let me tell you once again that I will leave today, and I'm sorry there's no way of saving you from dishonour." Puran left the room.

"There is…you're still a child, Puran Singh," Bare Bhaiya muttered under his breath.

"Pitaji," he said to his father, "there is only one way. We must send Asha away without Puran's knowledge. If he leaves there's no doubt he'll be miserable, but worse, the family will suffer dishonour."

"Where can we send her?"

"I say we send her to Kamla's. We'll explain everything to her so that she can take care of things."

"No, not at all! I don't want to cause trouble for my daughter. Send her off to her village." Mataji knew that her son-in-law, Karan Singh, had a ready appetite.

"Then let's poison the witch!" Pitaji said in exasperation.

"Try and control your temper, please."

"Arup is right. Kamla will take good care of her and Puran will never know where she is."

And so the Asha who had been brought here with such love and care was swept up and transported hundreds of miles away to Kamla's house. She was ashamed of what Kamla might think, but Kamla was not accustomed to thinking too much.

When little Sheela informed Puran that Asha Didi had left, he got up with the alacrity of a snake. First he went to the village, and then he came to fight with Bare Bhaiya.

"I understand everything… I knew from the beginning that you don't like your own sweet wife and have an eye for Asha…that's why you were so worried about her." Anger drives one to madness.

"Puran! What are you saying, have you lost your senses? Whatever I'm doing I'm doing for your well-being, otherwise if it were in my power, my dear brother…"

"Your power? What power you have used, Bhaiya! You severed my hands and feet, you've always been my enemy, Bhaiya…you must celebrate my death, you will inherit everything."

"Stop, Puran! Don't say things you will regret later. You're not just my brother, you're like my own son. If I wanted the estate I'd have arranged for your marriage without permission from Mataji and Pitaji so that they could disinherit you. Puran, don't think of me as

someone so low, please, for Pramatma's sake, don't break my heart."
Arup's sombre eyes filled with tears.

"But where did you send her, tell me where she is, I beg you."

"I didn't send her anywhere, she went away of her own accord. She said she didn't want to ruin your life—Puran, she's a goddess, she also said she would die rather than have any contact with you."

"Bhaiya, why did she say that? Doesn't she love me any more?"

"No, Puran, that's not it, she's a goddess, didn't your hear me? She left you because she loves you. Listen…"

"But what will I do now, Bhaiya?" Puran mumbled like a child.

"You're a man, you shouldn't weep for a woman. She's gone, but she didn't take your reason and common sense with her, did she? Immerse yourself in the affairs of the estate, finish preparations for your exam."

"But I'll seek her out."

"You'll only cause her more pain, Puran."

"Pain? Ahhh." Puran broke down and started sobbing.

You Forgot

The world forgets. A knife wound heals and the thought of pain slips from one's mind. While giving birth a mother vows she won't have any more children and wishes she were infertile. The moment her pain passes she croons over the new baby, and before long she is yearning for another child. But Puran's forgetting was a proper forgetting. Asha's dead. They say the plague took her. The whole village was swallowed by the plague. Even a wrestler like Ranji was not spared; his old mother's back is broken. Asha died, and Puran's desires died with her. He forgot a great deal. He forgot to laugh. Munna was older and had become so naughty, and a second baby now clung to Bhabi's breast, but Puran had forgotten how to show his affection for them, to tickle them. If Asha were there he would have remembered everything. He would have shown people that he wasn't a coward, that he had more to his name than Pitaji's money;

he would have shown them that there are many ways to live in this world. But why did Asha die? He even forgot Bhola's aunt. She tried to tease him herself, he smiled wanly in response and remained silent. The old woman's heart ached, she wilted.

"Puran, it's Sheela's birthday," Bhabi said in a playful tone, "what will you give her?"

"What shall I give her?" Puran asked, lowering his head.

"Let me see—here, Sheela, what would you like?" She whispered something in Sheela's ear.

"Auntie, right Mummy, auntie?" Sheela chirped.

"Yes, tell your uncle…"

Puran got up quietly and left the room.

"Why don't you marry, look how unhappy Mataji is." It was Bhaiya's turn.

"Yes, Bhaiya, everyone is unhappy on my account."

"That's not it, Puran, the doctor says marriage will improve your health."

"What? Bhaiya, marriage is not some medicine that can bring the sick back to health, and who said I was sick?"

"Puran, my dearest," Mataji said, placing his head in her lap, "will I take this longing with me to the grave? I have two sons, and one won't be married while I'm alive?"

For a while Puran said nothing. Who knows what emotions crowded his heart. He wanted to put his arms around his mother and weep. When he was a child and she took something away from him, this is what he did and she returned whatever she had taken. But It was death that had taken Asha away.

"My precious, your father is also getting old. Don't you think he longs for your wedding?"

The word 'wedding' stirred old memories; he remembered so much. But what a strange thing a mother is. She might cut you up into little pieces but you are, after all, a part of her body, and there was so much love in those eyes.

"Mataji, if you had any wish to see me married…"

"Puran, let bygones be bygones. A mother's mistakes are part of motherhood; it's maternal affection that makes a mother nurture her child with her blood, it's that same maternal affection that makes her destroy that child. But is she a demon? Son…" Tears flowed thickly from her eyes. "Do you think I'm happy?"

"Mataji, please, don't…"

"Say yes to marriage. When I see that you are happy I'll live a little longer, or else…"

"Do what you want, Mataji." Puran got up and went to his room. For some time he lay on his bed. Then, assailed by discomfort, he opened his drawer and took out the flowers. They were the same flowers, red, red like Munna's cheeks, red flowers that the earth had yielded, the very earth that had swallowed Asha. The flowers were black now, like congealed, dried blood.

When Puran's proposal arrived for Kamla's sister-in-law, everyone was jubilant.

"Do you hear, Puran is like our very own son," Kamla's mother-in-law, who had always looked down her nose at Kamla's family, said lovingly.

"Yes, Mataji," Kamla said, "Puran is such a pleasant person, just like our Shanta."

"Yes, do what has to be done." The old woman was trying to hold back her excitement.

~

"Forgot, you forgot so soon, Puran Singhji," Asha said, falling to the floor of her little room.

If only she were in her village so that, like Ranji the wrestler, she too could have been consumed by the plague!

Flames

There is one kind of fire that burns day and night in a hearth, and then there's another kind which is ignited when someone foolishly sets dry thatch aflame and you can see everything flare up in a flash like paper. Now we hear there are fires caused and spread by bombs, fires that, within moments, demolish large dwellings.

But the little spark which, deeply embedded in hot ashes, smoulders slowly, that too is fire. It does not burn down any large mansion or house but the hot ash around it gradually becomes lifeless from its slow heat. And if such a spark finds its way into the heart and hides there, the body eats, drinks and performs other functions, but that slow warmth and that sweet pain make you restive.

Asha was helping with Shanta Bai's dowry but her heart, like her hands, was shrouded by the light and shade of memory. God knows, it wasn't that she had ever wanted Puran to lose his sanity, nor had she wished that he would remain single in her memory. She did not deliberately fall in love, and when she did she didn't expect to be patted on the back or congratulated for it. But still—what did she want? Even when she was alone she could not admit to herself what she wanted.

Puran could have done something, he would have said something; she wasn't so far away, she was at his sister's house. She did not know that sometimes what we long for is right beside us but we still can't have it.

"Asha, look you've got the cloth hanging here." Showing her a piece of fabric, Shanta jolted her out of her reverie.

"What? Oh, yes, Shanta Bai. That's the way the fabric is—I did my best."

"Your best? Nonsense! Stitch it by hand now. Your heart's not in any of this." Shanta flung the fabric at Asha and left.

"Oh, Asha Devi is sewing." Sham Lal's manner when he spoke to her was always ingratiating. She didn't know what it was that made Karan Singh keep him on. True, he was intimidated by Karan Singh and perhaps that's what Karan Singh found appealing. He was a distant relative no doubt, or at least pretended to be, but now his position in the household was that of a poor relative. When Asha arrived he treated her with deference, but whenever he found her alone he regarded her with sweet, timid eyes and conversed with her in a honeyed tone.

"So you're angry with us, Asha Rani."

"Munshiji, why should I be angry with you?" Asha replied with a scorn that was worse than anger.

"But you turn away when I talk to you. Asha Devi, do you know what's going on in my heart?"

"Munshiji, will you go or shall I call Kamlaji?"

"Hai Ram, such cruelty! Is it a sin to talk?"

"Why don't you talk with Shanta Bai if you're so fond of talking?"

"Oh my—well, but Asha Devi, I'm a poor man and it's not my habit to reach beyond my means…"

Sham Lal had heard the story about Asha.

"Have pity, Munshiji, or is there anything else you want to say?" His fake sarcasm drove Asha to tears.

"Well, all I'm saying is that people should tread their own paths. Why climb over high terraces and end up falling on your face?"

"Yes, you're right, Munshiji."

"So, Asha, what if I talk to you."

"Munshiji, there's something else… I…why don't you go from here?" Asha felt lacerated by his sugary voice.

"Yes, but now Shanta Bai is getting married and I've heard her groom-to-be is very good looking, isn't he?"

Sham Lal was very clever, but he presented a dumb exterior so that he often managed to say something extremely meaningful, making it slide down your throat like a lump of sugar so you would never know what hit you.

"There'll be two or three people accompanying Shanta Bai when she leaves for her in-laws' house. Why don't you go, too?"

If she could, Asha would have stuck the dog's tongue with needles. Instead she just sat there with her head lowered, but after he left she could not hold back her tears.

The wedding day arrived. Kamla's carelessness was not something new; there were many things that didn't come in on time, several sets of clothing that still hadn't been finished with gold and silver lace. As if she were a machine, Asha was entrusted with putting the finishing touches on the clothes.

The wedding procession was fit for a king; for hours the columns of people on foot kept approaching, then the elephants and horses appeared. Crowded together in the window with some of the other girls, Asha too was watching the show unfold.

"Get out of the way, you witches," Shanta Bai pushed some of the girls aside and stuck her head out.

"You get away, girl, we won't let you see the barat. Have you ever heard of a bride clamouring to see her own barat?"

One of them said: "Well, Shanta is a child. When I insisted on seeing my barat, my uncle picked me up in his lap and took me to the window."

Another said: "And then the groom appeared on an elephant looking like a doll; you couldn't even see his face because of the way he was bundled up in fancy clothes!"

A picture of curiosity and interest, Shanta looked anxiously for his face. And Asha? That face had never been far from her vision. The wedding procession turned a corner and all the women ran to the other window. Lost in thought, Asha remained where she was. Where was she to go, anyway? Slowly her head fell on the window sill and she began to breathe heavily.

Away from the hustle and bustle of the wedding ceremonies, in a broken-down part of the house, Asha lay quietly on a small cot. For a long time she had vacillated between sleep and wakefulness; her heart sank, then seemed to receive a blow from somewhere, and she would awaken. The circling of the bride and groom around the sacred fire had already taken place. Fire-crackers and bombs were going off. Suddenly Asha felt at peace. Everything was done. As long as the ceremonies had not been completed she had nursed a tiny hope. But now that too was shattered. Her steps took her towards the door. What harm was there now? Had her eyes committed a crime that she should not see anything? And who would notice her in all the commotion, who would recognise her?

Quickly, keeping out of the way of the ropes extending from the tents, stumbling, she ran. The hall glittered with lights. The bride and the groom were seated next to each other. Tearing her way through the throngs, she found a place from where she could at least see Puran clearly. Forgetting everything, she had come to look at the bride and groom with the curiosity of a child. But the golden diadem looked so beautiful on his pale forehead, he was like a fairy prince! Asha had never seen him dressed in anything but his usual black and gray clothes, she had never seen him in such fancy, glimmering attire. He was a strange Puran today, so changed. Man takes on so many roles in the course of a lifetime. Sitting next to him was Bhabi, blooming like a flower, holding a bowl of water. Some kind of strange ceremony was in progress; the bride and groom were competing to see who was cleverer, who could find and retrieve the ring from the water. Puran had won several times; actually, it was Bhabi who was guiding his hand as if he were a child.

Right in front of the door, in a small clearing, a dance was in progress. Today, after a long time, Chamki was dancing. As soon as the ceremonies ended, people turned their attention to the dance. The crowds thickened.

Outside, fire-crackers were going off. A sparkler came and fell near one of the curtains which, along with a part of the door and the decorative paper cut-outs hanging from it, began smouldering. Chamki appeared drunk; her eyes flashed, and under the lights her cheeks glowed like flames.

Perched on a stool, Asha was trying to look over people's shoulders. The fire was surreptitiously advancing, low on the ground, and soon the carpet too was ablaze. The dance continued with the frenzied pace of death, like a pigeon fluttering its wings before being dashed to the ground. One of the girls tried to climb the stool on which Asha was standing. Asha lost her balance and screamed. The stool was quickly stabilised, but the game was ruined. Puran's gaze plunged into Asha's eyes and she became numb.

"Asha!" Puran sucked in his breath like a madman, like someone who sees a ghost approach from the cremation grounds and loses his senses. But within seconds Asha's stool tipped and she fell, just as if she had dropped into the very grave she had emerged from. A combination of shock and surprise made Puran's face turn a deathly shade of yellow. He stared wildly at that portion of the wall from where, moments ago, Asha's sorrowful face had slipped a message into his eyes and disappeared.

"Puran, what's the matter?" Bhabi shook his hand.

"Asha...just now..."

"What are you saying, Puran? What kind of silly talk is this?"

"Bhabi...she was here just now...she was here."

"Puran, don't act like a child. How can she be here?"

"But Bhabi, this was no dream, she was right here," Puran said in a strangled voice. "She's not dead, Bhabi."

"Puran, my dear brother, don't be a child. She may be alive or dead, but think, speak softly," Kamla cautioned.

"But, Bhabi..."

"No buts, Puran. What does it matter to you now if she's dead or alive? You're married and..."

"Married? But is she alive?"

"Puran, come outside with me, you don't look well." Bhabi tried to cover up the situation.

But the fire was blazing, flames leapt from the carpet, the curtains and the door, and Chamki... Chamki continued to dance. Flames flickered in her gossamer dupatta, but she was in a trance.

"Fire!" People started screaming. With one loud blast Chamki reeled, like a moth that flutters before crashing to its death on the flame, and then she fell on her face. "Fire!" Everyone saw her. Within seconds an electric wire caught fire. All hell broke loose. Puran glanced at Shanta's frightened face illuminated by the light of the flames. Overcome by the heat and smoke, she teetered. No one else was around and soon the flames were reaching up to the sky. Puran lifted Shanta in his arms and advanced in the direction of the room behind them. He saw the flames rising above the electric wire. He turned towards the veranda. Once again, in the halflit darkness, his soul retreated from the world and found itself in the cremation grounds. Withdrawn from the tumult around her, resting her head against a wall, was Asha.

"Asha!" Puran whispered hoarsely.

Asha was stunned. But not for long. Seeing Shanta in Puran's arms she began once more to sink into the river of despair; every fibre in her body became taut, the hot fumes choked her breath.

Puran put Shanta down and she watched these two with surprise; she too had heard some of the gossip.

Puran moved slowly. He was certain this was Asha's ghost which had risen from the earth for the purpose of turning the wedding parade into a funeral pyre. Afraid that she might disappear into thin air, he advanced cautiously.

"No!" Asha cried, clasping the wall. And Puran's being was touched to the core by this cry of anguish. Gently he touched her shoulder, sure that she was a figment of his imagination. But when his hand felt Asha's cold body he awoke.

"Puran." Sham Lal's voice fell into his ears, telling him he was alive, but Sham Lal hadn't seen the ghost as yet.

Puran made up his mind in an instant. Picking up Asha in his arms, he came out onto the veranda.

"Asha, you can't leave me now," he said, clutching her to his breast. "Tell me, was this a conspiracy? Now I understand, now I know! But the game is over. Asha, let's run away from this vile world, let us go." He made his way hurriedly along the line of trees.

Asha was lifeless like a puppet; Puran held her gingerly as if she were a child, a precious toy he had lost and found with great difficulty. She had slipped from his hands and was lost. Now he had dragged her from the cremation grounds.

"But wait, Asha, wait a moment. Bhabi and her children, I wonder if they are all right, wait here for me, I'll be back soon." He propped her up like a doll against a tree and left.

Puran battled with fire while Asha struggled with water, that water which is more forceful than fire and which will dislodge a solid rock from its place.

Sham Lal had been following them. As soon as Puran was out of sight, he approached Asha.

"I see, this is indeed a fine plan. Well, Asha Devi, you must be congratulating yourself for snatching the morsel right from the mouth." Who knows what Sham Lal was made of; no matter what the situation, his behaviour remained the same.

"Rani dear, this is all very well, but the sacrifice is not right."

Asha lifted her head at the word "sacrifice".

"This sacrifice of Puran Singhji's life—this is a rather high price to pay."

Asha said nothing.

"Have you thought about the fact that he is married?"

Asha felt as if someone had axed her, but she did not move.

"He's married, and his life is now tied to Shanta Bai's... Shanta Bai...what has she ever done to you? How strange that a woman oppresses another woman and then charges a man with the crime. Just think, Asha Devi, what will happen now? You'll go with Puran Singh, but where? Far away from the love of his mother and father, deprived of his inheritance? And you think you're so valuable he will forsake the whole world for you? And even if he does, you're also a woman..."

Once again a storm was brewing in Asha's breast, the same storm in which a great many weak people are swept away.

"And what will you get? You will only be known as a whore."

That was something Asha had not thought of.

"You'll be like a whore who forced Puran to lose everything." Finding that his argument was taking effect, Sham Lal became more forceful.

"Asha Devi, I know you're a goddess, a devi. Listen, although I'm a fool, I'm better informed on the ways of this world."

"What should I...what should I do?"

"Leave this place right now. If you go away Puran will never be able to find you. He was told you are dead. He will create a commotion, but if he doesn't find you he'll settle down eventually. He's a simple person, such a person can't be trusted. It would not be at all strange if he were to tire of you, too. If you go away he'll not remember you forever. Hadn't he forgotten you already? He was getting married, wasn't he? Listen to me, in a few days he will have forgotten you again. If you don't believe me, test him."

Asha got up. "I'll go."

"Yes, you'd better hurry, there's the road, it will take you to a village, it's not far, you can take a train from there to your village. Do you need money?" Sham Lal handed her something from his wallet.

"Remember what I have said. If Puran doesn't forget you, you can hit me a hundred times with a shoe, all right? I'm doing this for your own good, hurry up now, before someone comes along."

Struggling through thorny bushes, avoiding ditches, Asha ran. In the distance she heard Puran's voice. "Asha, Asha!" He was calling her. She stuffed her fingers in her ears and clenched her teeth. The fire had turned cold, but the embers continued to smoulder.

Peace

If you grind something and dust it off, does it disappear? You whitewash the walls, but in no time the paint is peeling again. You put a silver coating on the brass, but before long the silver wears off and the brass is only brass again. And here's a wound, you swathe it in bandages, but does it cease to be a wound? Yes, it ceases to be a wound, it festers and turns into a sore instead.

Unable to find Asha, Puran stumbled and fell. And he fell at the right moment, or else he would have found himself taking the road on which Asha was dragging herself. The commotion resulting from the fire, the upheaval of emotions and the force of the fall he took on the cold earth on such a chilly night—all of this reduced Puran to a state of inertia which lasted several days. His fever, his headaches and the weight of his family's anxiety seemed to clog his brain like smoke rising slowly from a charcoal fire. Ahh, how foolish he was! He had become such a nuisance. He reviewed his behaviour again. Was there any difference between him and a madman? And so he decided that he would fall into the terrible chasm called the world and cease to offer resistance. He no longer trusted his own judgement, and he was tired of the ever-recurring lectures. Letting go was a source of such peace, he could feel himself becoming completely submerged in it.

Whatever medication was given to him he accepted willingly; when someone made him laugh, he laughed, and when he was asked to sit, he obeyed. And thus, led by others, he began to live. It was as if he were floating alone in a calm, quiet river.

"Puran, why don't you read something," Bare Bhaiya suggested one day, and like a dutiful child he settled down with a book. Who knows how much he read. What an interesting book that was, what a great deal of information it contained!

Flowers, red, red flowers, fire, the frigid earth and buried in it that simple, pale face. Those sad eyes, the cremation grounds and that funeral pyre!

"Puran, you're reading the dictionary?" Bhabi asked in surprise.

"Let's play something, Puran, let's play a game of carom."

How the striker hits the checker, Puran mused, and whoosh! it falls into the pocket. And the striker is off again, racing across the carom board. 'Got it!' Black and white checkers, one that's red like a drop of blood—there, that's gone, too.

"You silly boy! You're hitting my checkers," Bhabi said, laughing. But then her eyes fell on Puran's lost child's face, and she became sad.

He's like a checker that's forced into the pocket by the striker and then retrieved and replaced on the carom board. When a person is cremated, do the ashes drift away from the cremation grounds and return? And does she stare at him again with tired eyes? And why were they giving him one drug after another? Oh…he was sick. He must be, or why else? After all, people must have his good at heart or they would not be making him take all this medication. How everyone loved him! And his wife? Oh, he had forgotten about her. He had circled the sacred fire with her at his side. That's right. But he didn't know what to do with her now. She was his wife, so what should he do with her? That's right, he will go to her tomorrow, yes, definitely and then, and then, he will go to her…they had walked around the sacred fire, hadn't they?

But the memory of circling the sacred fire made his head spin. Why had they gone around the fire? Once he had longed to walk around it, he had even teased Bhola's aunt that he wanted to marry her. Bhola's aunt. Like the black and white checkers she had fallen into a hole and, along with her tattered garments, she had been burnt. But these souls return from the cremation grounds, and those loving eyes become suspended in the air right next to you, the same quiet, shy eyes which once chattered impishly with you.

Why did he go and sit by the carom board last night? Why did he stare at it? Unseen hands twirled the striker, hit the checkers with it, making them fall into the pockets while he watched silently. And how sweet their faces were, just like the faces of Bhola's aunt, Chamki, and Asha. Asha, who was afraid of a baby frog, the timorous, frightened young girl!

And he would go to the drawer and open it, the drawer where those flowers still lay, the colour of congealed, dried blood now, but within seconds they burst into flames.

Chamki's face, the one Puran had last seen glowing like embers, would dance among the flowers and he would fall into a chair, upturning it as he sank into it. And then, for no apparent reason, Shanta would start sobbing and he would be given more drugs, but there was peace. Complete peace, the kind of peace that sits upon the undisturbed waters of a putrid, stagnant pond. Peace, silent and weary like death.

Stubbornness

For a few days Shanta continued to be bashful, but gradually she started giving Puran his medication and said a few words like, "Lie down," "Get up," "Eat something." However, she said no more than this nor did Puran understand any more. He was not mad; he ate, he drank, he dressed. But every once in a while he did develop a fever, cough or headache. This was the extent of his illness. If he were deranged would he not turn violent? The same Puran, who at one time thundered like a cloud and stormed, was now a docile person. And people still complained? Did he ever harm anyone? Could he ever harm anyone?

"Puran, why don't you talk to Shanta?" Finding him in good spirits one day, Bhabi ventured to ask. This was the same Puran and she was the same Bhabi.

"Me? Oh…but I do, Bhabi."

"Listen. No man mourns in this manner. Women have the prerogative to jump onto the funeral pyre and burn, but a man must stand firm even when he is crushed from all sides. The rules are not the same for all of us."

"Bhabi, why should I be mourning? I'm married, everything has been done. It's just that I don't feel very well."

"No, you've been sicker than this in the past. And you're not really sick, you're only imagining all this. Puran, just look at Shanta, see how unhappy she is. She has a heart too, you know, and you never say a word to her."

"Me? I speak to her, Bhabi." Puran indeed spoke to her, but what Bhabi was referring to was something else. After all, why was Shanta unhappy? All any Hindu wife wanted was to have a husband, and she had a husband. So what other goodies did she require? He was not a philanderer, he wasn't absent from home at night, he didn't hit her, didn't sell her jewellery in order to buy alcohol, didn't have eyes for other women, so what spiritual anguish was he causing her? Why did she go about looking like the very soul of suffering? A woman is a dissembler by nature. Especially those women who think they have inherited the right to consider themselves pure and chaste. But wait until the husband becomes old or sick; the treatment meted out to him is reminiscent of the way a butcher treats a cow whose milk has dried up. These are the women who, at the slightest pretext, turn to prostitution and then ask for the world's sympathy. What a good custom that was when they were burned like bugs on funeral pyres, or else the world today would have been overpopulated with prostitutes.

Puran was punishing her, but this was such a Mahatma Gandhi-ish punishment that no one had the gall to reprimand him. They had forced him to marry, but making him laugh or cry was not something they could control, and actually he was sick. As he lay slumped on the cold earth on the night of the wedding, a chill enveloped and bound his whole body and now that chill had travelled to his lungs.

"If a person doesn't feel very well, how can you expect him to laugh for no reason?" Puran said evasively and pulled the blanket over his head.

"It's up to you, but you should pay some attention to her. She was at her mother's for almost three months and you…" Bhabi knew Puran was not listening to anything she was saying.

"Shanta, watch over Puran, my dear. Do you see how lost he looks?" Bhabi played her other card. Shanta lowered her head and remained silent. If there was sap in the leaves, would things not have been altogether different to begin with?

"The doctors have assured us there's nothing to worry about. A stubborn man always likes to have his way, it's just a matter of a few more days. You should try and talk to him."

"Bhabiji, he doesn't reply when I say something, it's as if he hasn't heard me. And if I speak too much he covers his face with his blanket. You don't know him." Shanta was a woman and all the weapons she had at her disposal she had used already. She wasn't a man so she wasn't going to climb onto Puran's chest and force him to listen to her.

"There's a letter from Mataji." Puran was silently looking at some pictures in the newspaper. Shanta treid to distract him. "She's written that we should come for Holi."

Puran was gazing at a picture of a goat balancing all four hooves on a small peg. Animals have more gumption than humans. "Hunh," he mumbled, whether in response to Shanta's query or as a reaction to the picture, who could tell.

"She'd like you to come also. She's written that we should both go." Shanta felt like screaming.

"Should I go alone?" she continued patiently.

"Hunh, hunh," Puran nodded.

"You're…always like this…what I have done to you that you should hate me so?" Shanta could no longer hold her tears in check.

"I… Shanta… I." He was frightened by her tears and dropped the newspaper in alarm.

"It's not my fault that my parents burdened you with my person, but…" Her voice cracked.

"What are you saying? Shanta, I'm not well," Puran said shamefacedly. How could Shanta continue crying before a man who was so easily frightened? After she left, Puran returned to the picture of the goat. Suddenly he was engulfed by feelings of anxiety; leaning his head against the back of his chair, he sat unmoving for a long time. In the evening he developed a cold following an attack of sneezing.

What, after all, was the matter? He thought long and hard, but he was unable to come up with an answer. Finally he gave up thinking. The moment he focused on a thought his head swam. So he had chosen peace. What pleasure there was in this peace; we are lying here in contentment while people are tossing on live coals.

"Oh dear, Shantaji is hiding in her room again. Always hiding, isn't she?" Mahesh came in unnoticed and startled Shanta. She dried her eyes hastily.

"Ram, Ram! Tears? Are you crying, Shanta? There, I'm not speaking to you." Lowering his bulky frame into a chair, Mahesh grimaced.

"Why, you're always shedding tears… I agree that…but…" He muttered to himself. "I wish I could shake up Puran and throw him out. Shanta, do you know how I feel when I see you cry? My blood boils!" And indeed Mahesh had gallons of blood in his body.

"It's my destiny to weep forever," Shanta said wearily.

"What? What kind of destiny would that be? Get rid of it, throw it into the fire, I say. Listen, you create your own destiny, do you understand?"

"No one can create their own destiny, that's a silly idea, Mahesh Bhaiya."

"Whether we create a good destiny or a bad one is a matter of choice. But Shanta, I can't bear to look at your mournful face." Mahesh gazed at her fondly through half-shut eyes.

"Then don't look," Shanta retorted playfully.

"I shouldn't look? What a thing to say! As if it's in anyone's control to look or not to look."

"Of course, if you think something isn't nice you should…" Shanta turned her face away.

"Shanta, are you pretending or don't you really know what's in my heart?" The colour receded from Mahesh's face. "Shanta, how can I tell you, oh, you…"

Shanta continued to silently count the flowers on the cushion in her lap.

If on such occasions women respond wildly like flaming fire-crackers, you should be aware that the move has gone awry. And if there's silence, then that silence is just silence. Shanta didn't have enough gall to glow like a fire-cracker, nor was Mahesh foolish enough to scatter seeds on fallow land.

Was Shanta going astray, then? Who knows what going astray really means. Sometimes we go astray and, without being aware, digress from the crooked path to the straight one; often the difference between the straight and crooked paths is barely discernible. As a matter of fact, the paths leading to heaven are usually tortuous and thorny, while on a straight road a person stumbles and wanders like a blind man without a guiding stick, and what's funny is that he doesn't even know it. Why do people always strive for the straight path? Straight paths are frequently dull, well-lit and flat. Taking this route even a donkey, if it isn't disturbed along the way, will arrive at its destination. But these crooked paths, littered with unseen pits, hidden thorns, sharp stones, pain, heartache, where does one encounter these?

Shanta too was faced with two paths. One on which she was walking, on which she was rolling along like a true Hindu wife who worships her husband, as a good daughter, a chaste and pure woman, rolling along like a ball of loose dirt. Actually, like something worse. She had been burning in this cold funeral pyre for nearly a year. If only she, like Puran, were afflicted with a malady. She was afflicted, but what kind of affliction was this that constantly excited her being, making her body even more voluptuous, her eyes more unrestrained? Why did she quiver when she set eyes on Mahesh's body? Why did she feel as if that bulky figure was an engine threatening to crush her very being? But not crushing her so as to destroy her soul. Instead, it was like a pestle crushing a piece of sandalwood on a stone slab to make it more fragrant. Her soul, her mind, her heart were being pounded and poured into new moulds. Mahesh was not a philanderer, a profligate or an immoral person; he had never had a liaison with a low-caste woman, he had a wife and two children, and he was a family man. Then what force was this that pulled Shanta towards him? Just as your nostrils flare when the aroma of delicious food enters your nose and you inhale that fragrance so deeply it reaches all the way to your stomach, so the doors to Shanta's soul opened as soon as the sound of Mahesh's footsteps reached her ears. And she gathered into the depths of her heart his every utterance and every nuance of voice.

Just as Radha was compelled by the sound of Krishna's flute to forsake everything, pick up her pitcher of butter and run to him, so Shanta, driven by the same sacred and pure emotion, was driven to Mahesh. And like a burdened corpse, Puran was being drowned in oblivion.

Some things happen so slowly. The new moon appears silently, on tip-toe, like a tiny, insignificant thorn and gradually, a little bit at a time, it becomes a full moon. No one sees it grow. Puran's eyes failed not only to see the moon, they also failed to see the flames that blazed around his own person. And if he had observed the flames he would not have understood their significance, or perhaps he saw and understood but feigned ignorance. Who knows how many deranged people there are who, under the guise of madness, laugh at our folly.

Mahesh was not a scoundrel so he had no reason to be wary of Puran. He would sit with Shanta and talk to her for hours in Puran's presence. But he spoke to her in a language that only the discerning can understand. Puran didn't pay too much attention to them. And why should he have, anyway? Once, only once, he saw something that struck him as odd. Mahesh was helping Shanta take off bangles that were really tight on her wrists, and suddenly a bangle broke and made her bleed. Mahesh didn't do it intentionally, but Puran was surprised to see him bend over and suck the wound clean. His face resembled that of a hungry dog, and Puran felt he was going to suck all the blood from her body. But when he saw that Shanta, instead of looking pale and weak, seemed to have bloomed, he was relieved. Another time he was caught by surprise when he chanced to see Mahesh and Shanta in the drawing-room. Shanta had been lying on a sofa with her face down. Suddenly Mahesh flipped her over and then scooped her up in his arms as if she were a flower. True, Mahesh's hands were large and long, but…Puran examined his own hands; the skin was blotchy, and how crooked his fingers looked. He sat down on the sofa just to test something. First he gently turned the cushion upside down and then quickly lifted it up like a flower. His face glowed; slowly he put the cushion back in its place and gazed at it lovingly. He didn't like it when he caught his old servant, Lachman, staring at him oddly. Upset, he hurried to his room.

Puran's eyes had been blinded but others could see, and as for Lachman, he had eyes in his head that darted in all directions.

"Chote Bhaiya, there's something I've been wanting to say to you for a long time, I couldn't get a chance to say it before, but today I thought I'll say it," Lachman came and sat down at the doorstep.

"Hunh, what is it?" Puran said, counting the lines on the page before him.

"What can I say, master, don't you see? Don't you see how weak you've become?"

"Yes, Lachman, and I am taking my medicines regularly."

"Medicines? What medicines? I say something is wrong with Chote Bhaiya."

"What?" Puran was counting lines again. "It's the wrong medication? Well, why don't you suggest something then."

"You're asking me, master? Do you know what's happening in your home?" Lachman spoke in a loud voice.

"My home? Yes I do, Lachman, why?"

"Nothing! You know nothing!"

"All right, so I don't know. But is it necessary I should be aware of everything? And I admit you know everything. Now go and bring me some tea."

"Why not? If you won't pay any attention, someone else has to."

"Lachman, bring me some tea. And don't make it too strong, don't make it jet-black like you did the other day."

"Chote Bhaiya," Lachman spoke with restraint, "do you know that you and…"

"Lachman, bring me my tea!" Puran threw his book down on the table like a stubborn child. He wanted to scream. Lachman had no idea what was going on in his heart.

"All right, master, all right, but…" Lachman left.

How much can anyone take? One day Arup Singh arrived in Puran's room.

"What are you doing, Puran?" Arup Singh intended to stay for a while so he took off his coat.

"Me? Nothing really, Bhaiya," Puran assumed a jovial tone.

"Puran Singh, you've been married for nearly two years now, but there hasn't been the slightest change in your behaviour. The doctor says you're not sick."

"The doctor's an idiot, Bhaiya," Puran said with a smile.

"He says you're feigning, that is, you're superstitious. Puran, come to your senses. Lachman was saying…you're an intelligent man." He stopped suddenly.

"What was Lachman saying?" Puran was feeling better than usual.

"That…that…Puran, aren't you ashamed? You're a man, how can you tolerate all this?"

"Yes, Bhaiya, I'm a man. Who says I'm not? Look, these hands, these feet…" He extended his hands mockingly.

"Look, I eat, drink, what a big man I am, I got married and now, if Bhagwan so wishes…"

"Oh, Puran! Don't you have any shame?"

"Shame?" Puran broke into a laugh. "Why should I feel ashamed?"

"Listen, this has crossed all limits. I don't approve of Mahesh's visits and his association with Shanta."

"Why, Bhaiya?"

"Because Shanta is drifting towards sin."

"Sin? You mean because she's in love with Mahesh?"

"How easily you're saying this, as if it's no big thing," Arup said in surprise.

"If she loves Mahesh, let her, Bhaiya, please let her."

"Puran!"

"Listen, Bhaiya, she's in love, right? Let her be in love." Excited, Puran got up. "You have never loved, you have never loved in a way that…that you were consumed by it. You loved, but how? When Bhabi's love was delivered into your lap then you learned to love, and…"

"Isn't she your wife? Tell me, isn't Shanta your wife?" Arup felt he was losing ground.

"She's my wife according to the pandit's mutterings, but…"

"Then stop her!" Arup thought that wives were like bicycles that could be stopped merely by applying the brakes.

"Stop her? No Bhaiya, if I can't give her love, how can I stop her from asking for it from someone else?" Puran was changing his aspect today. He was speaking in a slow, deliberate manner, saying all the things he had been thinking about for a very long time. He sat down to catch his breath.

"You've gone mad!" Bhaiya thundered.

"Yes, I've been mad for a long time." Puran seemed bent on taking his revenge.

"The family's honour is not dear to you?"

"I have no honour or shame, Bhaiya. I have lost the capacity to feel. Nothing is dear to me anymore." He smiled bitterly and began drumming his fingers on the carom board. Once in a while, from the corner of his eye, he stole a look at Arup who was pacing the floor like a wounded cobra. Puran piled the checkers on the board. Today the feeling of victory was making him restless. He was taking his revenge with such passion. Sometimes a wounded sparrow innocently becomes the attacker. A calf must be sacrificed in order to ensnare a lion. Puran had given up his life in order to win the battle today—the calf lost its life but the lion was irrevocably snared.

At that moment Lachman came in and handed Puran a note.

Taking it up to the light, Puran read it. If you suddenly receive the news that India has gained independence, complete independence, and you've been chosen president, how would you feel? Or if the British hear that a large chunk has fallen off from the sun and landed on the entire German army, burning it to a cinder, and Hitler has been torn to shreds by a ferocious bear, how would they feel? That is exactly how Puran felt. But he wasn't a mean-spirited man. He read the letter silently, and saying, "Here, take this," he put it down before Arup and lit a cigarette.

His hands shook but a smile played on his lips, as if he had just received the disturbing results of an important exam.

"I'm leaving... I am nothing to you, but still...Shanta."

The paper fell from Arup's hands. It annoyed Puran to see that although it was his wife who had run away, it was Arup who was flustered.

"It happened finally...she left... Mahesh!" Arup held his head in his hands and shook from head to foot. Only he knew how he and his wife would be brought to task because of this incident. He glanced at Puran. In a flash the whole story unspooled before his eyes like a film reel: Puran's face which was like a blooming flower, his eyes wild with merriment that he longed to see again. He observed him closely: this was the same Puran, his younger brother, Bhabi's favourite brother-in-law, Amma's spoilt son, the children's beloved uncle. He had become a smelly, rotting dose of medication. If he hadn't been spoilt would he have been so obstinate? It was true that ever since his childhood he had been used to having his way and this was why he now clamoured for the stars in the sky.

"Shanta is an intelligent girl. Why would she have continued to seek pearls in a mound of dirt?" Puran broke the silence. He was attempting to curb his sense of victory.

"What are you saying, Puran? What has happened to you?" Arup didn't know what else to say.

"He's dead, your Puran has been dead for a long time. Now it's this dead Puran's turn. You can say whatever you want, Bhaiya, but the soul died ages ago. Now only this dead clay is present, if it can be of any help, please use it. But remember, Bhaiya, this body is hollow, there's not an iota of life in it." Puran smiled triumphantly.

"I…always regarded you as my child, Puran, and you talk as if I did everything deliberately…"

"But Bhaiya, have I complained? Whatever you did was all right. Not one but a thousand Purans could be sacrificed to save the family's honour." Puran hadn't forgotten how to be sarcastic.

"Puran, my child…" Arup choked with emotion.

"Bhaiya, what's there to cry about? Be grateful that the family has been saved from dishonour. However, your son is growing up now, just make sure he doesn't make the kind of mistake I did."

~

You can make any numbers of sacrifices, but God doesn't budge. Why does He have such an insatiable appetite? His stomach is like the pit of hell, it's never full. Every day He devours thousands, those sick from cholera, those chewed up by tuberculosis, still others dying from the plague. But nothing happens to Him; His demand remains unchanged, He does not even suffer from indigestion. Now, what had poor Raja Sahib ever done to harm anyone? Whose cow had he snitched that his daughter-in-law should run away? What crime had Arup's innocent wife committed that she should cry and go without food for four days and grey hair should suddenly sprout at Arup's temples?

Arup held his head between his hands. As a matter of fact, the whole family held its head between its hands; everyone was trying to make sense of what had happened. What now? What will be the fate of Arup's children? The family's name had suffered dishonour in the eyes of the sisters in-law as well. What a terrible thing this honour is; the more you serve it, the more difficult it becomes. A pox on it!

As if in vengeance, Puran became seriously ill. He spat blood again and again during the course of the day, and there came a time when all of them forgot about Shanta and tried instead to snatch Puran back from the jaws of death. The mother's forehead was lowered innumerable times at Bhagwan's feet and Arup, the commander-in-chief of the family, concentrated on protecting the castle. But the castle, it seemed, had resolved to bring destruction upon itself.

When I was a little girl I once saw a small shrub growing on the roadside. 'I'll plant it in my garden,' I said, and tried to pull it out with all my might. The weak and tiny roots shrieked, the trunk stiffened, but I succeeded in finally pulling out the shrub. The stubborn roots remained in their place. I brought the shrub home, planted it in my garden and nurtured it, giving it bucketfuls of water, but it soon dried up. Puran's family had also severed the roots, but just imagine their obstinacy! They were bent on replanting the tree and making it bear fruit. There is a special kind of tree that one can plant with its roots absent, but Puran was just an ordinary, weak plant. Then! Suddenly someone remembered the roots and a graft was suggested. Everyone convinced Arup to go to the village and bring Asha back.

After stumbling from place to place, Asha had finally found refuge in her village. When she returned to her old, crumbled dwelling, her first instinct was to set the house on fire and burn herself with it. But soon the people in the village got word of her return and her friends came running to greet her. She was assaulted by questions. She felt as if she had just awakened from a long dream. When she thought of Puran, it was as if she were thinking of the shiny moon stuck to the soaring heavens. She didn't like moonlit nights any more.

Ramu's mother once again began showering her with attention, while Ramu strutted about with his hair generously oiled. Asha observed his behaviour and remembered Puran's bright, untarnished face, his hair which was always clean and shining without the aid of cream or oil, his fragrant, unblemished hands. And here was this pickled, plastered down hair, hands roughened and afoul with the odour of cheap tobacco, and his vile desires! If a frog decided to make eyes at a nightingale, people would be sure to remark that the frog was out of its depth.

"Puran's condition has worsened," Arup said without mentioning the drama involving Mahesh and Shanta. "Mataji is alone and your Bhabi…" He blushed.

"Is Shantaji well, Bare Bhaiya?"

"Yes, but…for Puran's care…"

"I have no objection to coming, but Ramu's mother can't see very well and…" Asha was making excuses. If Shanta was there and certainly there was no dearth of servants, why did they suddenly want her? Someone eats the mangoes while Asha is left counting the leaves.

"Shanta is…at her mother's…"

"Oh? Is she…expecting?" Asha's heart lurched.

"Yes, that is, her mother is sick," Arup fumbled. "You come home with me and you'll understand everything. Asha—" he cut himself short.

When Puran heard that Asha was coming, he became inflamed. "How long are you people going to play games with me?" he muttered. "Won't you even let me die in peace?"

But Bhabi silenced him with a stare. In the evening his fever soared and he became delirious. "Such fire! Red, red flames…Bhabi, draw the curtains, these red flowers are like thorns in my heart…tell Chamki my head is swimming, tell her to stop dancing so wildly, tell her not to open my drawer, she's not coming back, why should she come back? Will I eat her up?"

He smiled to himself. "Such a frail little girl, Bhabi, don't make her work so hard, tell Mataji not to make her work so hard."

"Be quiet, Puran, the doctor says you shouldn't talk so much." He frightened Bhabi with his ravings.

"The doctor is an idiot, what does he know? The bastard, he won't let me speak. Bhabi, what will she say when she sees me? Don't tell her I'm sick, do you hear…what will she think?"

"Asha is here, Puran."

A flush spread over Puran's lifeless face. Bhabi was teasing him. The thought of Asha again filled his heart with a sweet and timorous feeling. He felt as if his dead self was being slowly tickled back to life. He glanced at his scrawny hands: how ugly they were! But why were his feet so smooth and healthy in appearance? He was disturbed by the sight of healthy feet attached to his thin, spindly legs; their roundness revolted him. He came to life when Bhabi left the room.

She was so naughty! He got out of bed and stumbled to the mirror. He felt as if the roof had caved in on him; skin and bones, a corpse from the grave, he looked like the dead body of a madman that had been propped up in front of the mirror. The mischief that had earlier danced on his face at the thought of seeing Asha confronted him now like a frightening ghost arisen from the cremation grounds.

He examined nature's handiwork closely. Cautiously he touched the veins in his temples and his neck. There were so many toiletries on the dresser, but there wasn't one thing among them that he felt he could use to adorn this corpse. He picked up the comb but found it impossible to struggle with his hair which had become thick and unmanageable. There was a sound at the door and he turned swiftly.

Asha saw the frightening vision and held herself back with great difficulty. But she ran forward when she saw him stumble. With his thin, reedy hands he grasped her like a hungry animal, his protruding ribs jabbed her chest like knives, but she summoned up all her strength and drew him closer to the bed. He thought she was trying to get away from him so he began crushing her savagely.

This was the same Puran whose slightest touch set Asha's body afire, making it glow. But today it seemed as though someone was enflaming her body by lashing it with icy whips. Forgetting everything she clung to him without shame. The time for modesty and diffidence was over. She embraced his bony, lifeless hands, and placing her head on his hollow chest sought some signs of warmth there. She felt as if an engine inside that skeletal frame was being set in motion; stifled, choked heat, a quiet tumult like molten fire inside a volcano that snarls like a wounded cat, and then violent tremors which seemed to have decided to upturn everything. In one jolt all order became chaos, the molten lava burst and, startled, she stood up. Her head was swimming, she felt she had been swung around several times and then flung on a flat plain. She didn't try to steady herself. Instead, she quickly went to the door and bolted it from the inside and, picking up the bottle of massage oil from the table, she gulped down its entire contents. Coughing and spitting, she quickly tidied the bed.

Then she pushed all the chairs and tables around the bed, pulled out clothes from the closets and spread everything on the chairs and tables. As she slipped her hand into the middle drawer of the dresser she felt she had been stung by a snake; the dessicated red flowers were still there, wrapped in a white cloth. She picked up each petal lovingly and arranged the flowers on Puran's chest. After this she picked up the night lamp from the window-sill and sprinkled kerosene from it on the clothes that were strewn around the bed. Then she climbed onto the bed like a new bride. Ahh...there was no time for modesty. She was not even repelled by the wetness of the lifeless blood that had trickled down his chin. She felt as though someone was raking her heart with sharp nails. Her hands shook. She put a lighted match to the kerosene that surrounded them and lay down in Puran's embrace, next to the dried out flowers that danced on his chest like a bed of red tulips.

ALSO BY ISMAT CHUGHTAI FROM WOMEN UNLIMITED AND SPEAKING TIGER

A VERY STRANGE MAN
(*Ajeeb Aadmi*)

'In this novel, Chughtai—whose reputation as a celebrated and controversial icon of Urdu fiction rivalled Manto's—told the story of the Bombay film world of the '50s. There hadn't been a more dramatic and candid account of the tangled emotional lives of Bollywood before this. There hasn't been another since.'
—Jerry Pinto

'*The episode of the sleeping pills was covered up. Dharam's condition was attributed to a case of indigestion. Zarina arrived with bouquets of flowers. Smiling.*'

This brilliant translation of Ismat Chughtai's original Urdu novel *Ajeeb Aadmi* is the riveting story of Dharam Dev, the famous actor, director and producer, and his all-consuming and doomed passion for Zarina Jamal, the young dancer from Madras whom he brings to Bombay and transforms into a charismatic actress. He looks on in anguish as his betrayed wife, Mangala, a well-known playback singer, sinks slowly into alcoholism. When Zarina abandons him, he is overwrought and dies of an overdose, friendless and alone.

In an interview, Chughtai described this novel about the Bombay film industry as a story based on the life of a producer-director who killed himself after the dancer he had made into a star left him in the lurch. 'I go into why he commits suicide,' she said, 'why girls run after him and producers like him, and the hell they make for these men and for their wives.'

This irreverent, sharply observed narrative of infatuation and ambition is vintage Chughtai.

'A delightful, bold and no-holds-barred novel that rips off several saris and dhotis as it twirls us around the cinema industry of the 1940s and '50s…This novel is a gem.'
—Kishwar Desai, *The Indian Express*

ISBN: 978-93-88070-79-9
www.womenunlimited.net www.speakingtigerbooks.com

ALSO BY ISMAT CHUGHTAI FROM WOMEN UNLIMITED AND SPEAKING TIGER

MASOOMA

'This book was not written for the faint hearted…A gritty anger and a biting realism combine with a keen eye for detail, not merely to depict the dark underbelly of Bombay [cinema] but also to scratch the mask of sharif culture.'

—Rakhshanda Jalil, *Biblio*

'People are of the opinion that she came to Bombay because one can get a good price for everything here…enthusiastic patrons pay generously. Whether it's old cars or jewellery belonging to the mistresses of noblemen, sons capable of procuring jobs, or attractive daughters—all fetch a higher price in Bombay.'

Set in the film world of the 1950s, this powerful novel may well be regarded as a work that celebrates all the talents of the legendary Ismat Chughtai—a writer who was brave, frank, provocative, entertaining even when she told the darkest of stories, and impossible to ignore. It traces the journey of Masooma—the innocent one—a young woman from a once wealthy family of Hyderabad who arrives with her mother in Bombay to become a star, but is soon embroiled in a game of exploitation, lust and treachery. She is transformed into Nilofar, a commodity that can be easily bought and sold; and in an effort to survive brutal and rapacious men—producers, actors, pimps and procurers—the mother and daughter descend into a world of corruption and moral decay themselves.

'[Chughtai's] writing is ironic, caustic, frank, bold, yes, irreverent…She is merciless in her depiction of corruption, deceit, injustice and hypocrisy. Yet, her empathy for her characters is always evident, as is her pain for their suffering.'

—*The New Indian Express*

ISBN: 978-93-88070-81-2
www.womenunlimited.net   www.speakingtigerbooks.com

Lightning Source UK Ltd.
Milton Keynes UK
UKHW020916100822
407113UK00011BB/2305

9 789388 326865